MAKE YOU MINE

FIREWEED HARBOR SERIES

J.H. CROIX

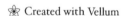

Chapter One

HAVEN

With my boyfriend, Rhys, working late, I'd settled in for the evening. I had a glass of my favorite wine and my laptop on my lap. I felt like I was finally catching my stride again on rebuilding my online business for artsy cards and invitations.

I planned to keep my extra job as a barista for the time being, primarily because I wanted to build up a cushion of savings for myself, but I also enjoyed it. There was an ebb and flow to the busyness of every day when I was there. I also felt like it was helping me get my groove back with returning to my hometown. Fireweed Harbor, Alaska, was a bustling small town, and it had been a full decade since I'd lived here. It was nice to be in the pulse of town at the café.

I cocked my head to the side as I adjusted the layout of my website. My business, With Love, had nearly crashed and burned after my ex-boyfriend stealthily re-routed my earnings into his bank account. Like an idiot, I had trusted him to help me. After almost eight months, my stock of handmade wedding invitations and other cards was building again. I had expanded into offering digitized cards for larger orders and had established a solid presence on several of the artsy online websites.

I enjoyed plunking around on the backend of my website. Today, I was uploading a line of stickers. I hadn't realized stickers could be a booming business, but I'd designed a few on a whim and discovered people loved them.

Although I spent many nights over at Rhys's place, I tried to spend enough nights here so that I didn't trick myself into thinking we were further along as a couple. I felt like we were in a good place, but I needed time, and I wanted to take it slow. We lived next door to each other, so it made taking things slow a little challenging sometimes. Our re-meeting last summer happened after I mistook his place next door for mine. The mini cape-style houses matched with dark gray siding and plum trim on the outside, giving a cheerful touch. The downstairs was open and airy with light-colored hardwood flooring and a peaked ceiling with windows that looked out onto a street that offered a view of the town's harbor.

My lease was due for renewal this upcoming summer, and I wondered occasionally what to do about that. Rhys was my landlord. He'd pointed out time and again that he didn't consider himself my landlord. His family's property management company, a tiny branch of his family's international corporation, technically handled my lease. I kept reminding him that he was the CEO of Fireweed Industries, a billion-dollar corporation. Fireweed Industries was owned and run by the Cannon family. The Cannon family was Fireweed Harbor royalty. All because they started Fireweed Winery a generation ago and spun that success into many investments and expansions. TL/DR: my boyfriend was a billionaire.

Startled by a knock on the door, I eyed the door skeptically. After a moment, I uncurled my legs, sliding my laptop to the side before standing and padding to the door in my socks. I swung it open to find a woman standing there. She thrust a manila envelope at me.

"Excuse me?" I prompted.

The envelope was already in my hands. I had reflexively taken it from her.

"Consider yourself served," she said before turning and walking briskly down the stairs.

"For what?" I called.

She didn't answer, climbing in a car and driving off. I let out a sigh as I closed the door, locking it for good measure.

I walked over to the kitchen counter, sliding my thumb along the seal of the envelope to open it. Seconds later, I was staring down at some official-looking papers that were not addressed to me. They were for Rhys. The two small matching homes we lived in were next door to each other, so it was easy enough to confuse them. I'd confused them myself when I originally moved in.

Uneasiness slithered down my spine as I stared at the papers with a sense of mistrust spinning in my chest. These papers were a demand for child support, claiming that Rhys Cannon owed years of back support.

"What is this?" I whispered to myself.

I felt sick to my stomach. How in the hell could he lie to me about the fact that he had a child? Even worse, trying to avoid paying child support? It wasn't as if he couldn't afford it.

I couldn't even read anymore. With fury driving

me, I stuffed the papers back in the envelope, put on my shoes, and marched out the front door down the walkway to Rhys's place. I knew the combination to get inside, and I punched it in quickly.

Practically stomping into his house, I placed the innocuous manila envelope on his kitchen counter. This was the end for us. I had enough issues with trust. I didn't need to try to rebuild this mess. With Rhys being my older brother's best friend and a fixture around our small town, it would be hell to avoid him, but I would deal with it. I had some pride to cling to and refused to be an idiot again.

As I walked back over to my place with my gut churning, I wondered if I should even explain, or if the papers he'd find when he got home would be enough of an answer.

Chapter Two

RHYS

I stared at the papers on my kitchen counter, genuinely confused. I knew the name of the woman requesting child support, but I hadn't seen her since college. As I read through them, I only got more confused. She claimed we had a sort of serious relationship. According to this bullshit paperwork, I'd been intoxicated one night and forgotten to use birth control.

I snorted to myself because I didn't get intoxicated. It wasn't that I didn't drink at all—hell, my family ran a brewery and winery, among many other ventures—but I never had more than one or two drinks, even in college. My older brother by one year had a serious problem with alcohol in college, and I'd been too aware of the risks to let myself stumble down that path. Jake had ultimately died from alcohol poisoning during his senior year in college. That was a lesson burned into my brain. The rest of us, all six of my siblings and me, didn't drink much.

I suppose that was remarkable, given that our

family's business started as a winery. Jake had reasons for drinking so heavily, and we all knew it. His life had been a god-awful tragedy. Even now, with him gone, I would've done anything to change what had happened to him, and I didn't mean simply the tragic circumstances of his death.

I knew Haven had to have delivered these papers to the house. She was the only person who had the combination to get into my house. She had to realize this was a bunch of bullshit, right?

I glanced at the time on my phone. It was after midnight. Crossing over to the kitchen windows, I looked toward Haven's house. Not a single light was on.

A sense of uneasiness churned inside me, but I decided to hope for the best. Surely, she knew this had to be a ploy for money.

———

"Haven," I pleaded. "This is not true." I held the cursed envelope in my hand, shaking it in the air.

Her green eyes had a hard look to them. "I don't know what to believe," she finally said. "And right now isn't the time to have this conversation."

She was standing behind the counter at Spill the Beans Café where she worked. I glanced around, my eyes taking in the curious gazes watching us.

We were at our small town's center of the universe —gossip central, where people came to get coffee, and the town's pulse.

"Haven—"

Haven Rivers had blown into my life like a fresh summer breeze. With her strawberry-blond curls, her pretty green eyes, and her lush, curvy body, I'd tumbled into lust for her last summer, quickly followed by love. As my best friend's little sister, I'd initially told myself Haven was off-limits, but I hadn't been able to resist her. A decade after I'd last seen her, the girl I'd hardly noticed in high school had blossomed into a stunning, bright spark that burned brighter the longer I knew her.

She shook her head. "Rhys, leave it alone."

"I can prove I'm not—" I began.

Her breath drew in sharply as she narrowed her eyes at me. "It says right in there she's willing to do a paternity test. Please leave me alone."

I felt a burning, sharp pain in my heart as I stared back at her. I'd gone and fallen in love with her, and now she was basically dumping me in front of everyone in town.

"This is not over, Haven."

"It is for me," she deadpanned.

As I walked out, I heard someone chuckle and comment. "Rhys might be a nice guy, but he should've realized his past would catch up with him."

I ignored the voice, pushing through the door and walking outside. I stopped on the covered porch, glancing around. The café was already preparing for spring even though the snow was still on the mountains and the air was chilly. No one was out here having coffee this morning, but the tables were out, and they had left the chairs stacked against the back of the porch.

It wouldn't be long before they would start putting out those heated outdoor lamps. I walked down the steps, pausing on the sidewalk, feeling uncertain about where to go. The indecision felt uncomfortable, and I shifted my shoulders as if I could shake the feeling off.

I always knew where to go—hook a right, angle

across the street, and walk to my office at the headquarters for Fireweed Industries.

Instead, I crossed the street and walked down to
the harbor. It was late spring, and the air was still crisp
and cold. Fireweed Harbor was nestled along the stunning coastline of Southeast Alaska. Mountains rose tall
behind the town with a glacier glittering in the
distance. The town's actual boat harbor was tucked
into a pretty little cove off the famed Inside Passage,
which stretched from Seattle to the Alaskan
panhandle and encompassed islands, coves, bays,
national parks, and fjords. Beyond its startling natural
beauty, it happened to be one of the few places in the
world where the water was deep enough for ships to
sidle close to the base of the mountains, offering up-
close views. It was truly a magical place, and I felt
lucky to be able to call it home.

I breathed the crisp, salty air gusting off the water.
This was my home, the place I'd come back to. Up
until last summer, I'd lived in Seattle, managing the
helm of our family's corporation from the headquarters we'd established there. Ghosts of the past, tangled
up in my brother's death and other messy details, had
set the wheels in motion to make some changes. For
years, I'd run from the memories that reminded me of
my older brother, but I didn't want to run anymore, so
I came home.

I'd stumbled into love with Haven, my childhood
best friend's little sister. That hadn't been on my bingo
card. And now, I had this mess to deal with.

"All I have to do is straighten it out," I said to
myself as I turned and walked up the dock.

I would call our family's attorney and get him to
kick this child support lawsuit to the curb. Then I

would fix things with Haven. She would realize I hadn't been hiding a huge secret from her.

Chapter Three

HAVEN

"You broke it off with Rhys?" Deacon asked.

"Of course I did!"

I ignored the tiny bit of defensiveness I felt inside. I hadn't expected Deacon to sound surprised. My older brother hadn't exactly been pleased when Rhys and I told him we were dating.

"Deacon, you're the one who warned me about him when we started dating. Rhys isn't exactly known for being faithful to anyone. You said he doesn't even get serious. I read the papers. He got her pregnant in college."

"Ok-aaay," my brother said slowly. "To your point, that's accurate about him not getting serious with anyone. But it doesn't add up. No matter what Rhys might think of this woman, he is *not* the kind of guy to blow off paying child support. He would want a relationship with his child if he knew they existed."

"Maybe he didn't believe it was his kid," I said, adjusting one of my earbuds.

"Maybe. Why don't you try having a conversation with him about it?"

"You're supposed to be on my side!" I protested.

Deacon was quiet for a moment. "I am on your side. Even if I agree that Rhys never used to get serious with anyone, he's not the kind of guy who would blow off his child. I think you can at least agree with that."

I grumbled before responding, "I suppose."

My brother chuckled. "Look, I understand this is stressing you out. I even understand deciding to put the brakes on this thing with Rhys, but it doesn't change how you feel."

I felt as if my brother had dragged a jagged knife across the surface of my heart. I swallowed. "What do you mean?"

"After you finally fessed up that you were seeing him, you swore up and down that he wasn't the guy to screw you over and that I needed to give your relationship with him a chance. Rhys told me he's in love with you. I'm pretty sure you feel the same."

"I don't see the point in talking about it," I snapped.

"Fine, we won't talk about it. I just have one more thing to say. I think a break is good. No matter what, this seems like a mess for Rhys to deal with. Let him sort things out, but maybe don't assume the worst in the meantime."

I spent two almost sleepless nights tossing and turning and assuming the worst. Two mornings later, I jogged down the steps at my house, studiously avoiding looking in the direction of Rhys's house. I failed in my attempt not to look, but my eyes bounced away quickly as I practically ran by. I loved this time of day. At ten minutes before five in the morning, it was quiet in Fireweed Harbor.

The small home I rented downtown was on a side

street off Main Street. When I turned onto Main Street, I glanced toward the harbor. The sun was rising, the early rays angling upward and casting a golden shimmer across the harbor waters. The morning air was salty and chilly this spring morning even though the higher elevations in the mountains still had snow. Some of it would remain through the summer.

My gaze arced in the other direction and traveled down the mountainside. Nestled into the feet of the mountains, the houses in my hometown peeked out through the evergreen trees. The winding roads were visible through the trees, and the downtown area was cute and colorful. Fireweed Harbor was situated along the famed Inside Passage of Alaska, a beacon for cruise ships and tourists. The town catered to them all year long, with spring through autumn being the busiest time of year.

My gaze made its way back to the harbor. Although my mood was anxious and unsettled, the fresh air gusting off the ocean and the colors of the sunrise shimmering on the water tugged my lips into a little smile.

An eagle called nearby, the sound sharp and piercing. Motion caught my eye, and I glanced over to see the eagle coming into land on one of the dock pilings. I scanned out past the boats in the harbor to see a small raft of sea otters gathered just beyond the docks. I took a deep breath, the air soothing me.

Turning away, I kept walking until I reached Spill the Beans Café. I strolled around the back, entering the kitchen and slipping the keys into my purse. After hanging up my jacket and leaving my purse in the break room for the staff, I tied one of the café aprons around my waist. The café's logo was emblazoned on it in shimmery pink with spilled coffee beans underneath.

Although I was tired, coffee was only moments away. I was relieved I had somewhere I had to be. It was hard to focus on my designs right now. I needed the distraction of customers and people keeping me busy all day long.

At five o'clock, I was the first one here, although I expected Hazel to arrive any minute now. She and Phyllis owned and run this place together. They'd been best friends since college and were now both widows. Hazel usually handled the morning shifts, and Phyllis took over in the afternoons. I was their main employee, and a few high school kids rotated after-school shifts and picked up the extra slack in the summer when it was insanely busy.

I loved this time of day here. I could putter around in the back and enjoy the quiet start to the day. I turned on the ovens and slid some premade muffins and savory rolls in to heat. I made my way out front, checking supplies for the coffee maker and espresso machine, and set out the day-old baked goods that we sold for a reduced price.

Once everything was ready and I had the computerized tablet register powered up, I walked to the door to flip the sign to open. After I unlocked the door, I turned on the decorative lights around the windows.

"Good morning!" Hazel's voice reached me as she came in through the back.

I glanced over, giving her a little wave. "Good morning." I began my usual loop around the front of the café, taking the chairs off the tables and setting them on the floor.

A few moments later, I rounded the counter and

rested my hips against it, smiling over at Hazel. "You made me coffee."

"It's my job," she said with a wink.

"Not technically."

This was our morning routine. Hazel insisted on making the first coffee every day. She handed a mug over as she began making her own in the espresso machine. She knew exactly what I liked—a triple shot Americano with just a little bit of milk foamed on top of it.

I took a swallow, closing my eyes as the caffeine jolt hit my system.

When I opened them, she asked, "How are you?"

I shrugged. "Okay." That was kind of a lie.

She tapped the button on the espresso machine to start her cup of straight-up espresso and rested her hips against the counter, mirroring my pose as she eyed me. "I heard."

I groaned. She let out a little sigh, a slightly worried smile curving her lips. Her blue eyes crinkled at the corners, and she lifted a hand to smooth it over her hair, which was pulled into a tidy bun.

"How in the world did you hear?"

"I heard yesterday afternoon. Rhys went to talk to their family attorney. I stopped by Fireweed Winery because our knitting group met last night, and we needed some wine and beer. Blake mentioned it. He said Rhys is totally stressed out."

Blake was one of Rhys's younger brothers. "I broke up with Rhys." I took a swallow of coffee, hoping the heat of it would soothe the tight, achy feeling in my throat.

"Aah. Well, Blake didn't mention that, but I'm sure that only adds to Rhys's stress."

"Well, he *should* be stressed out about this blast

from the past and the fact that apparently, he has a child out there who he hasn't even been paying child support for," I pointed out.

Hazel angled her head to the side. "Do you really think he would've done that if he'd known?"

Just then, the espresso machine beeped, indicating her coffee was ready. She turned away to finish getting it ready and prep the machine for whoever came in next.

When she looked back at me, I shrugged. "I don't know. I know that when I first told Deacon that Rhys and I were seeing each other, he wasn't thrilled. He pointed out that Rhys never got serious with anyone, which was true. I saw the child support paperwork. She's willing to do a paternity test." Hazel's eyes widened slightly. "Oh, so you didn't know that detail?" My tone was sharp.

"No, I did not. Okay, say it is his child. If she never told him, how is he supposed to know?"

I wasn't sure how to answer, so I simply shrugged. "I don't know. This whole mess aside, I just don't know if now is the time for me to stay in this. I think Rhys needs to sort it out. If he has a child..." I lifted a hand, letting it fall before my palm slapped on the counter. "He's like an instant father. He should probably focus on that."

"Have you talked to him?" she asked softly.

"A little. I told him we should take a break." I didn't want to admit that I hadn't really given him a chance to explain. I had trust issues, and I didn't need to try. I already had to overlook a lot when it came to Rhys.

Chapter Four

RHYS

"Dude, you've got some shit to deal with," my brother said as he shook his head.

I let out a groan as I rested my hands on the counter behind me. "Tell me something I don't know," I offered dryly.

Blake turned to face me, sliding his hips onto a stool across from me. We were in a back room at Fireweed Winery. This was where it all started for my family. Our great-uncle and aunt had started a winery and brewery. It had been small at first. Our great-aunt had enjoyed making wine for fun and decided to make a business of it because people kept telling her she was really good at it. She made wine and mead from the plentiful berries that grew wild in Southeast Alaska.

What started as a fun side business had exploded for them. It was a combination of good business sense, really good timing, and a delicious local product. The business quickly became highly profitable for them, and they expanded from making wine to brewing beer. Once they had more capital, they began investing it, mostly in Alaska, buying up land, other businesses, and more. They owned holdings in Southcentral Alaska, oil holdings along the North Slope, and several commercial fishery businesses. Time and again, their timing had been smart but also lucky. The business had expanded into an international investment company with holdings all over the world.

For a while, we had our headquarters in Seattle. We were that big. But a series of events had pushed me to make the decision to move our headquarters back here. We still had a small presence in Seattle, solely for when anyone from the company was passing through and needed a landing place. I was still dealing with the tangled mess that our corrupt grandfather had created. That alone had been enough for me to shut things down. He was currently in the middle of the sentencing process for felony embezzlement.

After the business grew, more family had started working for the company. Our great-uncle and aunt had passed away, and our grandparents were the only remaining family members from that generation still alive. I adored my grandmother, but my grandfather could burn in hell as far as I was concerned. Jail would have to suffice.

I was relieved to be back home, because between that and a tragedy that had blown up long-held secrets in our family, I needed to be back in Fireweed Harbor, back where I felt like we could somehow heal and move beyond some of the mess that had come to light.

And now this.

I looked over at my brother. We shared the same eyes, but he had darker hair and a more easygoing personality than I did. It suited him to be the one who ran the winery.

Blake leaned over, snagging one of the product

samples of a new honey wild blackberry mead. "Have one," he said as he handed it over to me.

I took it from him. "Thank you."

I glanced around the room at the stainless-steel counters and small bottling area. It was all for product samples. Several refrigerated cases lined one wall. Blake kept some of the product here for when he had tasting events twice a week.

Aside from hosting events and managing the store in this main flagship location, a warehouse attached to the back of it was where we produced the retail product. We tried to keep it exclusive so it wasn't too massive of an operation, but we were busy. We also had a restaurant attached to this, which was managed by the longtime chef who'd worked there.

"So what did Quinn say?" Blake asked.

Quinn Blackthorn was one of our family attorneys. Her grandfather had worked for our grandparents and her father for our parents. Her father was still working but had scaled back considerably. Quinn's offices were right inside our main office in the building beside the winery. We kept her busy, to say the least.

"She referred me to the attorney in their firm who handles family matters. I have a meeting with him tomorrow. Her quick take was if the woman is offering to do a paternity test, I should be prepared for the fallout." I paused and took a breath. "I spent a few weekends with Cathy, the woman filing for child support." I hadn't wanted to discuss that detail yet but knew I was only avoiding the reality of my situation.

"Oh fuck," Blake muttered. "Are you serious?"

I lifted a hand and let it fall. "Dude, there's no crime in having no-strings-attached weekends. I always used condoms."

My brother rolled his eyes. "I'm glad to know, but I

don't need that many details about your sex life," he pointed out.

I let out a short laugh, finally unscrewing the cap on the mead and taking a swallow. The subtle sweet berry flavor slid across my tongue. Lowering the bottle, I offered, "This is *good*."

Blake took a swallow from his bottle before grinning over at me. "Isn't it, though? We're always refining things. We haven't done one with blackberries in a while. It's a limited run, so we can charge a higher price."

"Smart plan," I replied before taking another swallow.

"What the hell are you going to do?" he asked a beat later.

"Take a paternity test, prove the kid's not mine, and move on with my life. Honestly, I'm not that worried about it. Well, I'm a little worried. Haven broke up with me."

"Over this?"

"Yeah. They served her by accident, instead of me. Quinn pointed out I could contest being properly served, but that's only a delaying tactic, so I don't see the point. Anyway, Haven saw the papers and everything. She said she wants to take a break and that I should figure this out."

"Oh fuck. I know you really love her," Blake offered.

My heart kicked against my ribs. It felt like my heart was actually angry with me. "I do love her. I feel like I should've seen this coming somehow."

"You said she's got trust issues, right?" he prompted.

"Yeah, her ex totally fucked her over. He stole her money and took off. He's the one who set up the backend of her website and everything for her business. She was close to broke when she got back to Fireweed Harbor."

Blake's brows hitched up, a look of disgust crossing his face. "Well, fuck," he said slowly.

"Yeah, and now it looks like I had a kid who I blew off and didn't bother to tell her about."

My brother studied me for a moment, taking a drag from his mead before lowering the bottle and spinning it between his hands. "You know, when you two started dating last summer, I was a little worried. Not about you, but getting serious was never your thing. I thought you might find yourself in a bind and piss Deacon off. Not that you have to answer to Deacon, but he is your best friend."

"I know. It's not how it worked out. Now, Haven's the one who dumped me. Do you think Deacon will get pissed off at his sister?" I asked dryly.

My brother chuckled. "Probably not. Go have that meeting with whoever Quinn referred you to and let the dust settle. This is kind of a big thing for someone to find out."

"I know, but it's not true," I countered.

"Are you sure?"

Chapter Five

RHYS

Are you sure?

Blake's question played on a loop in my brain later that night. I wanted to be sure, but the part of those legal papers that was accurate was I had spent a few weekends with Cathy.

"There's no fucking way," I whispered into the darkness.

I shifted on my pillows, tucking an elbow behind my head and trying to get comfortable. Sleep had eluded me for the last few nights. My mind spun back to those weekends with Cathy. I'd *always* used a condom because that was what I always did. She also said she was on birth control. Of course, there *was* a chance, no matter how slim. The part I kept questioning was why she didn't reach out sooner.

We had parted on friendly terms. The weekends we'd spent together had been casual and fun. She had no expectations, and neither did I. A niggling worry was I hadn't told her about my family and always kept the details vague. At that time, I wasn't the CEO of my family's company. I'd been in college, for crying out loud. So while I knew there was a possibility she could've gotten pregnant, I didn't believe it.

Are you sure?

Chapter Six

HAVEN

I held my hand out, reaching for the glass of wine Tessa had just poured me. She cocked her head to the side. "You've done the impossible."

I took a swallow of wine before asking, "What did I do?"

"I ran into McKenna, and she said Rhys is heart-broken." McKenna was Rhys's younger sister and friends with Tessa. I was friendly with McKenna, but we weren't as close. "If I was seeing someone and they got served with child support paperwork, well, that's kind of big news."

I looked over at my friend. I'd known Tessa Hensen since kindergarten. We'd easily slipped back into our friendship after I moved home and made a habit of getting together every week or so. Another friend from elementary school, Rosie Linden, was meeting us here as well.

The downside to a small town was navigating these tightropes. I knew the gossip about Rhys and me would spread like a brushfire in dry grass. It was all the more juicy because of the fact he was being sued for child support. The Cannon family was the subject of plenty of gossip in Fireweed Harbor. Aside from the fact they owned a billion-dollar corporation that put our tiny town on the map, their history contained tragedy with their father dying when the children were young, the eldest son dying in college, and rumors about abuse by their grandfather who'd stepped in to help after their father passed away. It was a lot to chew on as far as gossip went.

"How are you with all this?" Tessa asked.

I shrugged lightly. "Not great. I just think Rhys needs to sort things out. Whether he and I work things out afterward, I don't know."

Rosie approached our table. Tessa smiled up at her. "Hey." She patted the empty chair beside her. "For you."

Sitting down, Rosie smiled at us. "Sorry I'm late. Things were crazy at the hospital."

Rosie was a nurse at the ER department at Fireweed Harbor Hospital. Tessa lifted the bottle in the center of the table, promptly filling the empty glass in front of Rosie.

Taking a swallow, Rosie sighed as she set down the glass. "Thank God I'm walking home tonight."

"We can walk together," I offered since Rosie lived just a few houses down from me.

The server arrived to take our order. I loved our habit of getting together for dinner every few weeks. It was nice to be back home. We usually met somewhere downtown since the area was within walking distance for all of us.

After we ordered, Tessa leaned back in her chair. "No matter what, it's a messy situation."

"The situation with Rhys?" Rosie prompted. At my nod, she scrunched her nose. "It's a serious mess."

I let out a sigh. "I know."

Tessa shook her head. "Rumors are flying. Apparently, Rhys was involved with the woman who filed for child support for a short while. Did he tell you that?"

"Where did you hear that?" I asked. "And no, he didn't tell me. We haven't really talked. I got served the paperwork by accident, probably because my house is right next door and identical to his. I dropped it off at his place and told him I needed a break. That's it. I *do* need a break. Rhys is out of my league anyway. I have enough trust issues, to begin with. Anyway, what did you hear?" I tried to ignore the sick feeling building inside me. I didn't need to start obsessing over Rhys's past.

Rosie jumped in. "He actually came into the hospital lab for the paternity swab. I don't even know where that rumor started about the woman. He's from the Cannon family. Somebody's got the scoop somewhere. Whether it's accurate isn't the point. Even more complicated, rumor had it the woman was also involved with Jake."

Tessa grimaced, and I gasped. Jake was the eldest Cannon brother who'd died of alcohol poisoning in college.

Tessa glanced at me, her brows hitching up. "What do you want?"

"What do you mean?"

"For you and Rhys. Forget about this quagmire for a minute. What do *you* want?"

"I don't know. We've only made it eight months. In the large scheme of things, that's not too long. We weren't talking about marriage or anything. Maybe I really liked him..." I paused and took a gulp of wine to soothe the achy tightness in my throat and chest. I hadn't said it out loud, not to him or anyone. I almost couldn't let myself think the words. I had fallen in love with Rhys like the most foolish idiot in the universe.

"What I want, not specifically with him, but in general, is to have a relationship with someone who doesn't have secrets in their past and who isn't going to completely screw me over."

Rosie nodded emphatically. "Isn't that what we all want?"

"Can we talk about something other than me and that hot mess?"

"Sure thing," Tessa said. "Can we make a deal, though?"

"Sure, I think. What for?"

"We let you know about any rumors or gossip."

"Better for you to be prepared than taken off guard," Rosie added.

"Deal. Now catch me up to speed on your love lives," I teased.

Tessa burst out laughing. "I don't have one."

Rosie grinned. "Me neither. Should we start a 'we don't need a man' club?"

At one point during dinner, when the topic had been firmly diverted away from my failed relationship with Rhys, I got up to go to the restroom before we got the check. While I was in there, a woman came in. She was stunning with gorgeous, glossy blond hair. My hair was never glossy, ever. It was too prone to frizz. She had big blue eyes and a willowy figure. I'd never seen her before.

I didn't think much of it. After she left, Mimi Smith—a friendly but nosy elderly woman everyone in town knew, or so it seemed—met my eyes in the mirror. "That's her," she said.

"Who?"

"Cathy. The woman who claims Rhys is the father of her son. Smart move on your part."

"What do you mean?"

"Don't give her the time of day. She's nothing but a money-chaser." Her brows arched up as she tore the paper towel off and dried her hands.

Later that night, I curled my feet under my knees on the couch, idly flipping through the channels on the TV. If Cathy was that woman I'd seen in the bathroom at the restaurant, she was a clear reminder of why I thought Rhys was out of my league. She was the kind of woman he would date. She could be a model. I didn't think I was ugly, but my looks were less classically beautiful with my strawberry-blond hair that tended toward messy curls, my freckles, and my decidedly not-tall-and-willowy figure.

It was better for us to break up now than for me to fall even deeper in love with him. Even if doubts were clamoring to be heard in my mind, I wasn't going to be foolish. Again. If Rhys and I were to have a chance to work things out, he really did need to resolve the situation with Cathy. Despite his insistence that he didn't believe he was the father of her son, her willingness to do a paternity test kept the questions and doubts swirling in my mind.

Chapter Seven

RHYS

"Good to see you, Rhys," Colin Blackthorn said.

After a quick handshake, he gestured to the chair across from his desk. "Have a seat."

"I took care of the DNA swab at the lab yesterday," I offered as soon as I sat down.

"I heard. We should have the initial results in three to five business days. I requested the more in-depth analysis, which may take another week." Before I could ask why, he continued. "Meanwhile, I had a call from Cathy's attorney based out of Seattle. Apparently, she'll be here soon with her son."

Anxiety clenched in my chest. I'd been trying to ignore it, but this whole thing was stressful.

"Let me explain why I'm the guy who handles all the family cases. I don't mind being aggressive when my clients want to look reasonable," Colin offered with a light shrug. "I've mastered the art of being aggressive and assertive while making my clients look reasonable and friendly. Fortunately, in your case, this is a blast from the past. Your family has a lot of money, and I have no problem making her look greedy and pointing out that she did not notify you of her child for years. We've already done some digging. Were you aware she was also involved with your brother Jake?"

"What?" My tone was sharp and startled.

"Yes. On her old social media accounts are photographs of them at parties. She deleted it, the account that is, but we still found it. This is why I requested the additional testing. There's a possibility the markers could confirm you as the father, but extra testing can clarify if it's you or a sibling. She was seeing you and Jake around the same time. Was she aware of your family's business at the time?"

"Not from me. I'd like to say not from Jake, but I don't know. He tended to be private about it, but he also had a serious alcohol problem, as you well know. He died from it. I have no idea what he might've said to her when they were partying together."

"That's my concern. Of course, signs point to her finding out recently as she's only now reaching out. While we wait for the results from the paternity testing, we need to cover your bases. If this child is yours or your brother's, how do you want to handle the situation? Does your family want a relationship with the child? I'm assuming money is not a problem."

"If it's my child or even Jake's, we will provide financial support. Of course, if it's my child, I'd like a relationship with him. If it's Jake's, I know all of us will consider him part of our family." Pausing, I leaned my elbows on my knees and ran my hands through my hair. As I dropped them, I muttered, "Fuck."

"That's how we got here," Colin replied with a low chuckle.

I rolled my eyes, and a bitter laugh slipped out. "True enough." Leaning back in my chair, I asked, "What do you think she wants?"

Colin cocked his head to the side as he shrugged one shoulder. "Money, probably. I don't think she would be willing to do a paternity test if she didn't think the child was yours or your brother's. What was your relationship like with her when you stopped seeing each other?"

"I wouldn't call what we had a relationship. I was a junior in college, and we spent a few nights together. I wasn't looking for commitment, and as far as I could tell, neither was she. We parted on friendly terms. Or so I thought."

"What happened? My questions may seem nosy, but it helps me to know the context for how we approach things going forward."

"I understand. Nothing dramatic happened. We weren't exclusive. I met her at a party, nothing unusual about that, and we hooked up. I didn't see her for a weekend or two and then ran into her again. We spent a few more nights together, and that was it. The semester ended, and I came home to Fireweed Harbor for the summer."

Whenever I thought of my older brother, it was like a gust of cold air. Not the crisp, refreshing winter air but clammy, damp cold air. The kind that, if you stayed out in it too long, you were miserable when you came in.

"Jake died at the end of that semester," I added.

Jake's death was no secret. Anyone who knew our family in Fireweed Harbor knew Jake had died of alcohol poisoning in college. Some knew more. Specifically, that old rumors had turned out to be true—that our grandfather had physically abused him. Our grandfather had been an asshole to all of us.

Our father died unexpectedly from an epidural hematoma after a fall while he was out hiking. I still recalled the afternoon. He'd come home and appeared fine, but he had a headache. He went to rest and never woke up. I still missed him. After he died, our grandparents had been around a lot more. Our grandfather was abusive, and Jake had been his primary target. Unbeknownst to all of us until a few years ago, he had also sexually abused Jake.

That horrifying detail had only come out recently when our cousin Archer, who had witnessed it by accident once, finally told me what had happened.

It explained so much. Knowing that Jake had been my grandfather's main target for physical abuse, I had assumed that was the reason Jake drank so heavily. But there was even more behind it, and that knowledge was a painful splinter in the wound left behind by Jake's death.

While I had told the rest of my siblings and my mother what Archer saw, nobody in town knew that detail, not that I was aware of. The tragedy of Jake's death was enough as it was.

Colin's gaze was somber. "I'm so sorry about Jake."

I swallowed, taking a quick breath. "Thank you."

Colin was quiet for a few beats before he continued, "I'm assuming if you didn't know that Cathy was also involved with Jake that you have no idea the status of their relationship, or what kind of terms they were on?"

I shook my head. "Not a clue."

"I will let her attorney know that financial support is not an issue. I will also let him know we are aware of her relationship with Jake. I don't know if that'll change anything. I'll make it clear that the family wouldn't dispute financial support in either case."

"Is there anything else I need to do while we wait?"

He shook his head. "We wait. As soon as we get the results, I'll call you."

After I left Colin's office, I headed to my childhood home, where I had stayed for a little while when I returned to town. My mother had been traveling, but she was back in town now. Although I had told several of my siblings about the contact from Cathy, I had asked them to wait so I could talk to my mother privately. With this new information about Jake and his relationship with Cathy, I had more to carefully navigate.

I didn't know why, but I sensed Jake was the father. If my hunch was accurate, it would be a gut punch for my mother.

Chapter Eight

RHYS

"Rhys!" My mother held the door open and leaned up to dust a kiss on my cheek.

"How many times do I have to tell you it's not necessary for you to knock?" She tsked when she smiled up at me as I walked through the door.

"Habit," I replied.

"Come into the kitchen." She gestured for me to follow her as we walked through the open-style living room area into the kitchen. My childhood home was open and airy with a modern feel. The ample windows and earth-toned colors created a warm feel to the space.

I took a seat at the counter, sliding my hips onto one of the stools there. A charcuterie board with small sandwiches, slices of cheese, fresh vegetables, and meats sat in the middle.

"Anything to drink?" She tossed the question over her shoulder as she walked toward the refrigerator.

"Just water."

I took a bite of one of the triangular-shaped sandwiches. "Really good," I said after I finished chewing.

"It's smoked honey turkey with pesto and cranberry cream cheese. Simple but delicious." My mother put a glass of water on the counter beside me and sat down across from me.

I had another small sandwich and a few slices of cheese before taking a swallow of water.

"You said you had something to talk to me about," she finally said, her gaze expectant.

My mother's dark hair had liberal streaks of silver, and she had wide gray eyes. Age had graced her well with her features softening. Today, she had her hair up in an artful twist and wore a simple white cotton blouse with loosely fitted navy-blue slacks.

I mentally braced myself. "I did. I'm glad you're sitting down."

My mother, Clara, arched her brows. "Please just tell me."

"I've been served court paperwork for child support."

My mother's breath drew in sharply as her eyes widened. "Is this even a possibility?"

"It's a woman I saw in college, but not for long. The math would add up. I definitely used condoms, and she claimed to be on birth control. She's willing to do a paternity test. I've already spoken to Colin Blackthorn." Now came the even trickier part of this conversation. "His team has done some digging and discovered she was also involved with Jake around the same time based on her social media photographs."

My mother blinked, sadness passing through her eyes like clouds blocking the sun for a moment. "Oh," she finally said. "So if Jake was alive..." She began before closing her eyes and pressing her palm to her chest. She took a deep breath as if she could contain the pain of my brother's loss.

When she opened them again, I replied, "It was his last semester of college, my junior year."

Jake and I looked startlingly alike—same coloring, same height, and so on—and we'd often joke that we were twins. We were similar enough that people could've been convinced we were twins if they didn't know us well. We had been one year and seven days apart. I missed him so fucking much.

"How old is this child?"

"His name is Matthew, and he's ten. Cathy Miller is his mother. I don't know why she waited to share this. I already told Colin, obviously if the child is related to us, whether it's Jake's or mine, we'll provide support."

"Of course!" She drummed her fingertips on the table as she looked at me.

"I have no basis for this other than a gut feeling, but I think Matthew is probably Jake's and not mine."

She studied me quietly, the sound of her drumming fingertips coming to a stop. She laced her hands together, resting them on the counter. "I trust your gut. At least now that you're more mature."

"What's your point, Mom?"

She shrugged lightly. "Young men in college aren't known for their judgment."

That elicited a sharp laugh from me. "Fair point. As soon as I know something about the paternity test, I'll let you know."

"Is she in Fireweed Harbor?"

"Her attorney told Colin she'd be traveling here soon. We can certainly request to meet him if paternity shows we're related."

"Are we concerned she'll claim we were avoiding involvement?"

"We'll do our best to prove that if she resists any

contact. I'm prepared to fight. I'd prefer not to have to, though."

My mother took a quick breath. As was her way on sensitive topics, when she was done, she was done. She changed the subject abruptly. "And how is Haven handling this news?"

My mother adored Haven. I silently groaned. "She dumped me," I said curtly. "Unfortunately, the papers were delivered to her place instead of mine. I tried to talk to her, but she told me I needed to deal with this. Obviously, it's not a great look that it's possible I was hiding a child from her."

"Oh, dear," my mother said as she shook her head sharply. "I suppose that would be a surprise. Give her a little space. Once you know whether or not you're the father, fix it."

I let out a disbelieving chuckle. "I will certainly try, Mom. But I can't just wave a magic wand and make Haven believe me."

Chapter Nine

HAVEN

"Here you go." I handed a coffee across the counter, a coffee that was, as Hazel would describe it, a serious concoction.

It involved more than one flavor of syrup with skim milk frothed atop it, complete with a heart-shaped design. The woman quickly paid and walked away. She was the last in a burst of customers from the first cruise ship to visit Fireweed Harbor this spring. I began wiping down the espresso machine and tidying up behind the counter.

Hazel popped out from the back, smiling over. "We just made more in that last hour than we did all of yesterday."

I grinned at her. Spill the Beans Café was popular with locals and tourists alike. We did a brisk business for locals, but the cruise ships that came through town rained money on the businesses when they were here.

She handed me a small muffin. "Taste it," she ordered.

I looked down at the sugar sprinkled on the top

with visible bright berries. "Is it a new flavor?" I asked as I peeled the paper off the bottom.

"Yes," she whispered in a conspiratorial tone as she slipped her hips onto a stool by the espresso machine.

Before I took a bite, I glanced around the café. The tables were full, but nobody was in line, so I could take a mini break. Taking a bite, I closed my eyes and let out a moan at the burst of wild raspberries that exploded in my mouth, mingling with a subtle sweetness. Opening my eyes, I finished chewing. "Delicious."

Hazel gave me a satisfied smile. "I aim to please. I have a full batch coming out shortly."

Just then, the bell jingled above the door, and we glanced over together. The woman I had seen the other day in the restroom when I was out at dinner came walking through. This time, Cathy had a little boy with her. The moment my eyes landed on him, I let out a startled gasp.

When I glanced at Hazel, I knew she saw the same thing I did. This little boy was definitely related to Rhys. Cathy approached the counter. My mouth felt dry.

Hazel, bless her, saved me. Leaping up from the stool, she gave me a hard nudge with her elbow, asking, "Do you mind checking on the oven in the back?"

I absolutely did *not* mind and fled through the swinging door into the kitchen. I took several deep breaths, attempting to remain calm.

Ha! Who was I kidding? I was the opposite of calm. I felt a little sick. My breath was short, and my fingers tingled and were cold.

Like the biggest idiot in the universe, I'd gone and fallen in love with Rhys Cannon. I'd known better. Back in high school when I crushed on him, he was so far out of my league it was beyond foolish. I knew he was still out of my league when we ran into each other last summer for the first time, but he'd convinced me otherwise.

This woman, Cathy—I knew that was her name solely because I'd seen it in the paperwork demanding that he start paying child support—was the kind of woman I imagined Rhys dated. Tall, beautiful, with a willowy figure and cornflower-blond hair.

The sound of the bell chiming out front snapped me out of my negative train of thought. I'd frozen in place in the center of the kitchen beside the stainless steel table. I forced my feet to move. I was about to open the oven to check on the muffins when I realized a timer was set.

Of course, a timer was set. Hazel didn't need me to check on the muffins, but she'd given me a good excuse to hide in the back. I crossed the kitchen to the break room and staff bathroom in the back corner. I washed my hands quickly and splashed cold water on my face, trying to snap myself out of this judgy headspace.

I dried my face with one of the clean dish towels stacked on the shelf beside the sink. I took a moment to study myself in the mirror as I lowered the towel. My strawberry-blond curls were pulled up into a pony-tail, messy as usual. Several wayward curls had escaped, one pointing straight up and the others out to the side.

I blinked, and my eyes stared back at me, taking in the freckles scattered across my nose and cheeks. I had despised my freckles in high school. I'd grudgingly learned to accept them, but I didn't think I'd ever love them.

The mirror reminded me of what I already knew. I

was nothing like Cathy, not even a little bit. This was the reminder I needed. I'd gone and let my heart get reckless and make foolish choices. Even if this hurt, it was for the best.

Rhys and I had only been dating since last summer. Maybe that was a little while, but it wasn't like my last boyfriend. We had lived together for two years before I discovered what an asshole he was.

A tiny voice chimed in. *You can't believe Rhys would hide from a child. Maybe he used to keep things casual, but he's not that kind of guy.*

Shut up, my more strongly defined critical voice volleyed back.

I wondered what Deacon would say if he saw the little boy with Cathy. There was no doubt that child was a Cannon. After a deep breath, I turned and walked back out front, steeling myself to be friendly and polite to every customer who came in.

The second I stopped beside Hazel, she smiled over at me. I looked around quickly, my eyes homing in on Cathy and her little boy over at a corner table. When my gaze made its way back to Hazel, I said, "The timer says the muffins will be done in fifteen minutes."

Her eyes twinkled as she shrugged. "So they will."

Just then, the bell jingled above the door again, and we looked over together to see Rhys walking in. It felt as if the universe conspired against me. I wanted to flee to the back again, but dammit, I wasn't going to be a coward.

"I've got it," I said to Hazel.

"I'm sure you do, but I'm not leaving you out here alone," she said under her breath.

Rhys was within earshot by then, and she smiled brightly. "Are you here for your afternoon coffee?"

He stopped in front of the counter, his gaze lingering on me for too many beats of my heart. It felt as if I'd been running too fast already and was stumbling down a hill. I couldn't control my heartbeat and almost felt panicky. Cathy was here, and any second now, Rhys would notice her. It felt as if I was watching a car accident.

Hazel was saying something, but I didn't hear it over the static in my brain. I didn't mean to look over toward Cathy, but I did, and then Rhys followed my gaze.

I whipped my head back to look at him. His breath drew in sharply, and his face went pale. Hazel, skilled at navigating small-town gossip and awkward interactions between exes and the like, looked dismayed for a second before she schooled her expression to bland.

Rhys held my eyes. "Haven—" he began.

"We don't need to talk," I said quickly. "Maybe you should go say hi to Cathy."

"Haven, listen to me. I've already gotten the test results back. He's not my son. He's my nephew. We believe he's Jake's son."

I stared at him.

"Can we please talk?" Rhys pressed.

Hazel glanced back and forth between us. When she looked back toward Rhys, she said gently, "I don't think now is a good time." Turning to me, she added, "Go in the back. I will handle the counter. I need you baking."

My feet wouldn't move. She placed a hand on my shoulder, turning me and giving me a little push between the shoulder blades. I walked into the back, my brain trying to absorb what Rhys had just said.

What the hell?

Chapter Ten

RHYS

Hazel studied me before cocking her head to the side. "Your usual in the afternoon?" she prompted.

I *really* wanted to talk with Haven. I looked past Hazel's shoulders, hoping I could catch a glimpse of Haven in the back over the top of the door.

"I know you want to talk to her, but you'll have to wait."

I whipped my eyes back to Hazel and took a quick breath. "Okay."

"Your usual?" she prompted again, and I nodded. "Cathy is looking at you." She began prepping my coffee without once turning her head in the direction where Cathy sat with the little boy who I presumed was my nephew. The paternity test had ruled me out, but they had also revealed her child was related to me, closely enough to be a nephew.

"She just got the news that I am not her son's father," I offered.

Hazel studied me. "You said that. So you think that's Jake's son? Why would she even consent to testing if she knew that?"

"Remember how we used to joke that Jake and I looked like twins?"

Just saying that aloud made my heart ache a little. I missed my older brother.

Hazel nodded. "You and Jake looked an awful lot alike."

"She dated both of us. I didn't know that until Colin Blackthorn chased down some old social media posts."

Hazel passed me my coffee, and I immediately handed her the five-dollar bill I'd tucked in my pocket. "Keep the change."

"That is some serious 'cups up' news for this town."

I narrowed my eyes. "Hazel, please."

"You know I won't talk to anyone about this, but you should be prepared for the gossip. Hell, anyone who sees that little boy will make assumptions. Your best bet is to get the news out first. Otherwise, gossip will catch fire and burn someone in the process. You need to talk to Haven."

"I just tried to talk to her," I pointed out.

Hazel made the change from my five and stuffed the remainder in the tip jar, shrugging as she glanced back up at me. "You did. It's just now isn't a good time or place." She tilted her head in Cathy's direction. "I'm tempted to send Haven home for the day, but I don't think she'll agree to go."

"No," I said grimly. "She won't."

"Please tell Haven what I just told you about the testing. I know I said it, but I'm not sure she believes me. Don't tell anyone else. Well, other than Phyllis," I added, knowing it would be near impossible for Hazel to hide this from her best friend.

Hazel nodded, her gaze serious. She made the sign of the cross in front of her heart.

I took a breath. "And now, I will go say hello to my nephew."

I walked across the café, stopping beside Cathy's table. She looked up with a tight but polite smile on her face. "Hi, Rhys."

"Cathy." I dipped my chin." I'm assuming you've heard."

"I have," she said.

Her son looked up at me, and my heart experienced a jolt. He was wearing earphones. His eyes were so much like Jake's. Others might say they were like mine, but I didn't look into my own eyes very often. He looked back down at the phone in his hands, his thumbs moving over the video game he was playing.

She was quiet as she studied me. "It's not about the money, you know."

"I don't care if it is," I said bluntly. "Our attorney gave your attorney some times. When you all get back to him, I will see you then."

She gestured toward her son. "This is Matthew." He took out one earbud. "Matthew, this is Rhys. He's an old friend of mine from college."

Matthew looked up at me. "Hi," he said.

"Nice to meet you, Matthew."

Someone spilled a drink at a nearby table, snapping through the moment and creating a distraction. "Good to see you," I said when I looked back at Cathy. "Talk soon." I didn't wait for a reply, lifting my coffee cup in acknowledgment as I turned away.

Matthew's mere existence was stirring up so many emotions around Jake and the gaping hole he had left in our family's life. The relief I felt at learning I didn't have a son had quickly been replaced by a piercing sense of longing for my brother and to ensure that Matthew knew his father was a good man. Jake had been young when he died. He'd been flawed like we all were, but I hated that his life story was punctuated by such a tragic end.

I knew he wouldn't want people to know all that he had experienced at the hands of our grandfather. Yet it still ate at me. Our grandfather was facing charges for felony embezzlement in our family's company. We knew we couldn't ever hold him legally responsible for what he had done to my brother, but that had only been one of his crimes. The ugliest for certain. We could make sure he paid however we could. People in town knew he'd been harsh, but they didn't know the whole story. Even though Jake wasn't here, I wanted to protect him from the gossip that would circle like sharks around our family if the whole story came to light.

As if the mere thought of Jake set this in motion, my grandmother called as I was leaving, asking me to stop by. Since she lived near downtown, I aimed in that direction.

When I walked into the living room, my grandmother was seated in her favorite chair. Although she had plenty of money, she still lived in the house she and my grandfather had occupied when they started Fireweed Winery. It was nice enough, but it didn't reflect what she could have. It was a beautiful piece of property near downtown Fireweed Harbor, situated on the bluff overlooking the harbor. The view was a stunner, with a clear view of downtown, the harbor, and a few islands.

Her face was weathered, but her gray eyes were warm as she smiled at me. "I met Matthew," she said, her voice a little raspy.

"Mom told me." My throat felt tight as I sat down on the nearby couch.

"He looks like Jake. And of course you. Because you and Jake were Irish twins," she said lightly.

I nodded. "He sure does."

"You're doing right by him. I know we don't have to do anything."

"He's family. And even if Cathy is just after this for the money, Matthew is Jake's son. We'll take care of him."

My grandmother nodded before offering, "Do you want any coffee?"

"No, thank you. You said you had something to discuss?"

At her nod, I took a slow breath. For the past year, we've been dealing with an ugly situation—for our company and for our family.

"Clint has taken the deal."

"Okay. How many years?"

"Five."

My asshole, abusive grandfather had been verbally abusive to all of us, physically abusive to Jake and me, and had raped Jake. We didn't know that horrifying detail until my cousin Archer came forward with it. Archer carried his own trauma from witnessing it by accident once. We would never be able to hold our grandfather accountable for what he did to Jake, but since he'd also been embezzling from the company for years, we'd gone after that aggressively.

He'd accepted a plea deal for felony embezzlement. This was the only way he would answer for any of his crimes. Jake never told me about how bad it had been, and that still stung. I didn't hold it against Jake for not telling me, but I hated that he had to carry that alone.

I just wanted my brother to find peace, even if he was no longer with us. I wanted to somehow atone for what he'd gone through.

"I wish we could do more," she said.

"I do too," I said after a few beats. "We all do."

"I wanted to give you the update. I also wanted to ask that none of us go to the sentencing."

"No?"

She shook her head firmly. "No. When I became aware of how he treated you all, I wanted to remove him from the company. But I felt like it was the only way I could keep him in check. It was my leverage. I will never stop regretting that I didn't realize how bad things were."

"None of us did."

"But you were children. The reason I don't want any of us at the sentencing is because he'll hate that he's just that irrelevant to us. I wish the sentence was longer. It's enough that I hope he dies in jail."

I studied her for a moment before nodding. Considering I would have to keep myself from standing and driving my fist through my grandfather's face at sentencing, it was probably for the best that none of us went.

After I left there, I drove to the cemetery on the outskirts of town. I stopped in front of Jake's gravestone, reading the inscription. *Loyalty, friendship, and love. May his spirit live forever.*

I thought back to Jake, remembering how he had flashes of anger as we grew into adolescence. I chalked that up to life, to facing the wrath of our grandfather. None of us knew just how bad Jake had it. He must've felt so lonely. He'd protected us all. My most vivid memory was one time when I was trying to stand up for Wyatt. Wyatt had accidentally broken something, and my grandfather went to slap him. I stepped between them and took the force of the slap instead. At that point, Jake was taller than our grandfather. He had come in and stepped between us when my interference pushed our grandfather into a rage. My heart ached at the courage that must've taken, knowing what our grandfather had done to him.

Jake had been so loyal to all of us. I only hoped I carried his mantle well.

I placed my hand on the inscription plate, tracing my fingertips across it. "I miss you," I whispered. "I hope you know we all do."

Blinking my tears away, I took a deep breath and held it for a beat before I let it out and turned away.

I intended to walk back to the office, but I couldn't focus on work. My feet kept moving as I passed the main location for Fireweed Industries, turning into the entrance of the building next door, Fireweed Winery, the flagship store, and restaurant for our family's business. Fireweed Industries was so much more than this now, but this place was where it all started. Behind the store and restaurant lay the production and distribution warehouse Blake managed.

With Blake being a year and a half younger than me, we didn't have the level of closeness that I had with Jake growing up, but we'd become closer since I'd moved back to Fireweed Harbor. I wanted to bounce this situation off him, and I needed to talk with someone who loved Jake.

Chapter Eleven

HAVEN

I sat on the couch with my legs crossed while I stared at the fire in the woodstove. The flames flickered behind the glass door. I had tried to work on new graphic designs for some cards, but I couldn't focus.

I sighed, thinking about Rhys and Cathy and the news that he wasn't the father of her child. I'd ended up working late at the café because I told Hazel I needed to stay busy. She'd harrumphed about it and muttered her disagreement under her breath, but she'd graciously let me stay.

A knock on the door snapped me out of my reverie. My pulse instantly started to race. I glanced over at the door, wondering if it was Rhys.

I didn't like admitting it, but I missed him. Standing, I told myself not to be ridiculous. Maybe it was Rosie. Since she lived down the street, she stopped by sometimes. Last week, she had stopped by because she ran out of sugar and was baking that evening.

My heartbeat wasn't listening to my logic and kept on tapping out a wild rhythm. A few feet away from the door, I came to an abrupt stop, looking down at

myself. I was in my comfy clothes. The evenings were
cool because spring was chilly in Alaska. I wore a pair
of soft fleece pants that swung around my legs and
rested low on my hips. Atop that, I had on an old
sweatshirt, the fabric soft from years of wear. My fluffy
blue socks with stars on them were probably the most
fashionable item I was wearing if they could be considered fashionable in any way.

I'd pulled my curls back in a ponytail and reflexively reached up to tighten it on my head, smoothing a
few wild locks away from my forehead.

"What are you doing?" I whispered to myself.

Obviously not quietly enough because Rhys said,
"I can hear you, Haven. Please let me in."

I rolled my eyes, feeling my cheeks heat with the
embarrassment of getting caught talking to myself. I
tried to take a deep breath, hoping to quell the anxiety
spiraling through me. It was to no avail. The mere
sound of his voice set my heart to beating even faster.

On the heels of another shallow breath, I curled
my hand on the doorknob and opened it. A major
downside to avoiding someone was that your nerves
went a little haywire when you saw them.

I stared into his silvery-gray eyes. My brain
thought I said hello, but apparently not because Rhys
prompted, "Haven?"

I jumped slightly, blurting out, "Hi!"

His eyes coasted over my face. When we'd been
seeing each other, I'd discovered that having Rhys's
attention on me was intoxicating. He was a man of
detail and care. That attention could cut both ways.

Just now, I didn't like how perceptive I sensed he
was. It had taken so much nerve to let down my guard
and give him a chance last summer. Me, the quirky girl
in high school who'd crushed on him so hard. He was

my brother's best friend, handsome and popular. I'd hated my crush on him because so many girls liked him in high school.

"Can I come in? I was hoping we could talk," he said quietly.

"Uh, sure."

I stepped back, swinging the door open wider for him. He walked in, stuffing his hands in his pockets as he turned to look at me. My brain was lagging; everything was happening a few steps behind. A cool gust of wind blew through the open door. I belatedly closed it before catching the hem of my sweatshirt and rubbing it between my fingers.

If I was being honest with myself, which I preferred not to do, I knew avoiding Rhys forever wasn't practical. It also wasn't the best thing for my sanity. Yet it hurt to see him. After a shitty breakup with my ex-boyfriend—which maybe hadn't splintered my heart too badly but had left my pride battered and bruised—I'd come home to lick my wounds and try to rebuild my life.

Ending up next door to my brother's best friend and high school crush hadn't been on my bingo card. I also hadn't expected the chemistry that snapped and crackled in the air between us whenever we were near each other. I *absolutely* hadn't expected Rhys to try to persuade me he wanted me. Cynical me, I also hadn't expected to fall for him as swiftly as I did.

That was the problem with a man like Rhys Cannon. All of the things I didn't think I wanted—his handsome looks, his hair like honey gilded with sunlight, his silvery-gray eyes, and his muscled, lean, and rangy body. The man was freaking oblivious to just how handsome he was. It was all ridiculously unfair. To top it all off, he was a nice guy. I knew this because he was Deacon's friend. They had stayed friends all these years. Even after Rhys left town for a few years after college, he and Deacon played video games online and chatted weekly. I knew he was still the friend Deacon turned to when he needed advice.

Rhys was genuinely down to earth. His whole family was. They were very wealthy, but they didn't act like it. Two of his brothers were firefighters with Deacon up in Fairbanks. They were just a regular family who happened to be wealthy.

All of these thoughts tumbled through my head as I stared back at Rhys. I finally snapped myself into motion, walking past him and calling over my shoulder, "Do you want anything to drink?"

"Sure," he said in that rumbly voice of his that danced along my nerve endings, setting them alight.

I walked from the living room area to the kitchen at the back, feeling Rhys's presence as he turned to follow me.

"I have water and some honey blackberry mead from the winery. I think I have some porter from there too."

If you lived in Fireweed Harbor, you likely had wine, beer, or mead from Fireweed Winery. They had special prices for the locals. They were highly successful in the wine and beer-making business because their product was high quality and delicious.

"I'll take a beer," he said.

I fetched a beer for him, twisting the cap off before I handed it over, then got a bottle of mead for myself. I rounded the island that served as a divider between the kitchen and living room and walked back toward the couch.

Rhys followed me. I regretted the fact that all I

had was a loveseat. Either I made him stand or we sat together.

Gesturing to the loveseat, I said, "Have a seat."

I sat in the opposite corner from him, shimmying my hips back as far as I could. That only created maybe a foot or so between us. My belly spun from the butterflies.

He took a swallow of his beer and leaned forward, resting his elbows on his knees as he dangled the beer bottle between his hands. He angled to face me slightly, catching my eyes.

"Like I told you today, he's not my son. His name is Matthew."

I nodded slowly. "He's Jake's?"

"We think so. My attorney had the sense to request more than a basic paternity test, one that identifies more markers. According to the lab, he's related to our family and likely the child of one of my siblings." He paused, glancing down and back up. "I understand why you got upset."

I shifted my shoulders, trying to relieve the tension building inside me. "Maybe I overreacted," I finally said.

He shrugged. "A woman filed for child support from me. Surprisingly, there *is* a connection."

"Are you sure Jake is the father?"

"Based on what the lab explained, if we rule out my other brothers, then the only option would be Jake."

"How are you?" The question slipped out. Realizing Jake might be the father reminded me of how painful his death was for Rhys and the rest of his family.

Rhys took a long swallow of his beer before leaning back and setting the beer bottle on the table beside the couch. "I'm okay. I'm worried about my mom. She wants to get to know Matthew if he's her grandson. I'm not sure how Cathy feels about that."

"I'm sure this is difficult for her and definitely unexpected."

He looked over at me, his gaze intent. "We could talk about all kinds of things, but I'm hoping you believe me now. I wasn't hiding anything. I knew Cathy in college, and we saw each other a few times. Apparently, she was also involved with Jake right around the same time. We only found that out because our attorney did some searching before he even agreed to let me do the paternity test." His lips twisted to the side as he shook his head. "I wish I could talk to Jake about it now."

"Did she really think you were the father? Surely, she knew what the DNA testing would show?"

Rhys shrugged. "According to my attorney, it depends on how many markers the test looks for. He recommended the more expensive test specifically because of that. According to her attorney, she thought we were twins." Rhys rolled his eyes. "You know how we used to joke about that."

"I knew you guys growing up, so I knew you weren't twins, but I could see how someone who didn't know you well might think that. You sure looked a lot alike. Maybe not identical, but really close."

He let out a breath, shaking his head in disbelief. "Haven, can we try again?"

Chapter Twelve

HAVEN

I lifted my bottle of mead and swallowed too much, sputtering a little. I reached for a napkin on the coffee table, dabbing at my mouth. "Maybe," I finally said. "It's not just this. You never noticed me in high school for a reason, and I think this whole thing just reminded me of all the reasons maybe it was stupid to think we could work out."

He narrowed his eyes. "Haven, you were a freshman when I was a senior. That's kind of forever in high school. Not to mention you were and still are my best friend's little sister. Those were the reasons I didn't pay attention in high school. Four years is not a thing now, and Deacon knows how I feel about you."

I opened my mouth to argue the point. Rhys shifted closer on the couch, reaching for one of my hands. I didn't realize I was cold until his hand closed around mine. "You're freezing," he murmured. He stood and walked over to the woodstove, asking, "Can I add some more wood to this?"

"Sure."

He quickly added a few more logs, poking at the fire to get the flames leaping high. After he closed the door, he walked across the room, peering at the thermostat mounted on the wall. "Do you have the heat off? It's still below freezing some nights."

I felt foolish because I'd honestly forgotten to check the thermostat when I got home. "Go ahead and turn it up."

After Rhys adjusted the heat, he returned to the couch, sitting closer to me. My pulse thrummed along. Thoughts bounced around my brain. I tried to stay sensible, to tell myself that perhaps I had reacted too swiftly. But still, seeing Cathy and knowing Rhys had once been involved with her, regardless of the casual level of the involvement, had simply illuminated what I knew already. Rhys was out of my league.

He lifted his beer bottle, taking a long pull. My eyes lingered on the motion of his throat, trailing down to where the vee of his shirt revealed a glimpse of his bronzed skin. It wasn't even fair. Somehow, Rhys's skin stayed burnished, as if by the sun, even at the end of winter when spring was beginning to break through.

I tore my eyes away, my gaze landing on my forearms, which were pale and dusted with freckles like most of my body. I was fair-skinned, no matter the time of year. During the summers, I had to be religious about using sunscreen, or I turned pink.

The sound of a beer bottle being set on the table by the loveseat snapped my attention back to Rhys. He looked over at me, reaching for my hand again. Even though I told myself I should swat him away, I couldn't. I wanted to be angry with him. Instead, I was annoyed with myself for getting upset and tumbling back into my need for him so easily. That was all it took for me to start feeling weak inside, vulnerable to his charm and the ease he carried.

Some men worked to create the aura Rhys wore like a favorite old jacket. He didn't even have to try. I took a moment to study him. His hair was dark blond with glints of gold shimmering under the flames flickering from the woodstove as if the sun itself gilded him. His silvery-gray eyes were beautiful with thick lashes. His cheekbones were bold as if cut from granite. His jaw had sharp, clean lines set off with a generous mouth. He could look foreboding, except when he smiled. He had a dimple on one cheek that appeared with his smile, giving him an endearing, boyish look.

All of the Cannon siblings had good looks and easy charm. Yet I bet they'd all trade that. Jake's death had hit the family hard. My heart softened just thinking about what it must mean to realize Jake might have a son.

Rhys's thumb brushed across the back of my hand before feathering along the side of my wrist. His touch was subtle, but it felt like a lick of fire.

"Can we try again?" he repeated.

His low and gravelly voice danced along my frayed nerves. I lifted my chin, daring myself not to look away or back down like I wanted to.

Rhys was much easier to resist when he wasn't right in front of me. I opened my mouth to say something, but I had to take a breath first. Collecting myself, I swallowed. I gave up on trying to calm the pace of my heartbeat. It was like a wild pony out of control, dashing through an open field.

"I feel like we stumbled into this too fast. Maybe I

overreacted, but I saw Cathy..." I let out a little sigh, looking down at where his hand held mine. I wished I didn't savor his touch so much. Lifting my eyes to his again, I added, "I'd guess she's the kind of woman you usually date."

"Haven, I don't have a type."

My brows hitched up as I gave him a dry look. "Seriously, Rhys? I'm sure I could do a quick online search and find plenty of photos of you with gorgeous women at social events. You didn't get serious with anyone. And that's okay. I'm not holding that against you. But—"

He cut in. "But what? Cathy and I had a few nights together over the course of a few weekends. I was in college. I didn't know it then, but like I said, she was seeing Jake at the same time. We were young, and it was casual. There is absolutely *no* spark for me with her now if you're worried about that. You are who I want." He studied me, his gaze intent and earnest. "I get it," he said after a long pause. "I don't think you overreacted. Hell, if the situation had been reversed, I'd have been pretty freaked out. That would've been a big secret to keep *if* it had been a secret that I was keeping. Let's try again."

I wanted to resist, I really did, but the problem was I had already fallen for Rhys. That was a done deal as far as my heart was concerned. And no matter what my mind thought, our chemistry still burned hot and fast. When he shifted closer, lifting a hand to palm my cheek and turn my face toward his, anything my mind wanted to shout out was futile. All intellectual resistance went up in smoke, burned to ashes in the fiery flames of my own need.

"Can I kiss you?" he asked, his voice a gruff whisper.

Of course, he just *had* to go and ask, to push me to make a choice. My answer was a forgone conclusion.

"Yes," I rasped.

His hand slid down from my cheek to cup the side of my neck. His thumb trailed along my jawline, his touch like a path of sparks along the surface of my skin. Heat and desire pooled in my belly. I took a quick breath before he leaned forward, pressing a kiss on the side of my neck just behind my ear. A little something between a sigh and a moan escaped. His touch felt like a drop of honey, sweet and hot.

Because Rhys knew me, he knew how to kindle the fire hotter and higher inside me. He took his sweet time—another kiss a little lower on my neck, his thumb brushing across the wild beat of my pulse, and a hot, open-mouthed kiss just under the edge of my jaw. He lifted his head, his gaze dark as he stared into my eyes.

I couldn't have looked away if my life depended on it. It felt as if we were caught in a net of shimmering sparks. Desire curled around us like smoke, suffusing me and the air.

"I've missed you," he whispered.

Emotion rose fiercely inside me, like a wave crashing through me. "I missed you too."

It had been a mere month. Honestly, it was remarkable that I'd managed to avoid him so thoroughly for that month. But I had.

I *had* missed him so fiercely. I took a shallow breath just before he dipped his head and brought his mouth to mine, claiming me with a masterful, devouring kiss.

His tongue swept in the second my mouth opened. On a moan, his hand slid around my nape, gripping my hair just hard enough that I savored the subtle sting on my scalp as he angled my head to the side to deepen our kiss.

I couldn't get enough, and I whimpered as I shimmied closer. We broke apart to gulp in air, staring at each other.

Chapter Thirteen

RHYS

"Kiss me again," I murmured.

Haven closed the tiny distance between our mouths. Our kiss went from chaste to a fiery tangle of tongues. My tongue swept in to glide against hers, and I let out a little growl when she shifted closer. I could feel the soft give of her breasts against my chest just before we broke apart.

I released her hand, lifting mine to trail my knuckles across her nipples. They were tight little peaks under my touch through the fabric. I let my hand drop, sliding it down to cup between her thighs. She squeezed her legs together a little, letting out a whimper. "Rhys..."

She was wearing these stretchy fleece pants. I tugged the waistband down, sliding my hand into her panties to find her hot, slick, and wet.

Another whimper escaped when I slid one finger into her folds. With a little encouragement, she stood and shimmied out of her pants. "I need to see you," I whispered huskily.

I took off my shirt, letting out a satisfied sigh when she tossed hers aside and let her bra fall behind her on the floor. Her breasts bounced free, and I shifted, pushing my jeans down until my cock sprang free. Precum was already rolling out of the tip.

"Are you...?" She began.

"I need you." My voice was guttural.

She straddled me, and I brought her down over me. I notched my crown at her entrance, and my head fell back as she slowly sheathed me in her slick, rippling core.

When she was fully seated, I lifted my head, looking into her eyes. "I missed you."

She blinked, a tear slipping down her cheek. "I missed you too," she whispered.

"We're going to be okay." My words were a promise.

I rocked into her, nudging deeper with each roll of her hips. It had been too long. My release was right there, a fiery sizzle waiting to strike.

I knew her well now and could feel her torch song in the tightening of her body, the way she started to tremble, the way she bit the corner of her lip, and the way her breath came in sharp little pants. I slid my thumb over her clit, watching as her release broke, and she let out a ragged cry. I finally let go, that sizzle cracking like lightning through my system. I came with deep shudders wracking my body.

Haven rested against me, soft and lush in my lap. I wrapped my arms around her, holding her close. I savored the feel of her breath gusting against the side of my neck and let my fingers slide through her hair. I had missed her and all of these small moments. I cataloged the feel of her skin against mine, the way I could feel her heartbeat slowing in tune with my own when she started thinking and tensed slightly before straightening.

Chapter Fourteen

HAVEN

I needed this. I needed Rhys.

When it was all over but for the pleasure rico-cheting through my body, he held me close against him. I wanted to regret this, but I couldn't even do that. I had simply missed him too much.

Oh, I could blame it on this man playing my body like an instrument solely tuned by him, but it wasn't just that. It was the way I felt when I was with him and the depth of our intimacy. Those were the reasons I'd let myself fall for him. I had been *so* susceptible to falling for him.

His fingers sifted through my hair, and I savored the feel of his easy touch and the way he didn't shy away from us.

"Haven."

I lifted my head from where I had it tucked into the curve of his neck. When my eyes met his, my entire system felt the jolt of it, the power contained in his intent gaze.

"Well?" he prompted.

"Well, what?"

"Can we try again?"

Chapter Fifteen

RHYS

Haven stared at me, her lashes sweeping down before lifting again. I hated the indecision I saw in her eyes. If only she knew. This past month had been hell. Facing the uncertainty surrounding the paternity test while Haven ignored me had been rough.

Finally having Haven back in my arms where she belonged sent emotion rolling through me in waves. My heart kicked along my ribs, each beat an echo of my certainty for her, my love for her. The feelings I hadn't put a voice to yet.

That was where I'd dropped the ball. Because I'd never been serious with anyone. All of Haven's brother's hesitations about me had turned out to be true. Deacon knew me well. He knew what I'd been like before I'd fallen for Haven.

"I thought that's what we were doing," Haven finally replied, lifting a hand and sifting it through her messy curls.

Her curls had fallen in a wild tangle around her shoulders. The flames from the fire and the woodstove danced along them, catching threads of gold in her strawberry-blond locks.

My lips curled into a smile. "Well, we started to try again, but I don't just mean this."

My hand had come to rest on her bare hip, and I caressed her silky skin, squeezing gently and savoring the soft give.

She took a shuddery breath. "I know. What do we do next?"

"I take you out on a date."

I had actually thought this through. I was going to court her. We weren't going to rush into this. We *had* rushed into it before, and maybe that was why it'd been so easy for that court paperwork to create doubt for her.

———

A while later, I lay in the darkness, wide awake. For the first time in a month, my thoughts weren't chasing themselves like a dog chasing its tail, pointlessly going nowhere and catching nothing.

I wasn't under any illusions that everything had been resolved. I still had a knotty mess to deal with regarding my nephew. I also knew Haven's hesitation was grounded in a piece of reality. She was wrong about the type of woman I wanted. Maybe Cathy was classically beautiful, but long before I had fallen for Haven, I'd been more drawn to quirky, curvy women whose beauty stood out. Cathy would blend into any crowd while Haven stood out with the brightness of her strawberry-blond curls, the way her smile was a little crooked, and the sharp intelligence contained in her gaze.

I slid my hand down her back. She was curled

against me with one knee draped over my legs. I slipped my palm down her silky-smooth skin into the dip of her waist and over the curve of her bottom. Even now—perhaps an hour or so past feeling utterly sated after we tumbled into bed together, and I teased her to another climax before finding my own again—my arousal stirred. That was the depth of power she held over me.

I could never resist spending a night with her. That part wasn't about sex. It was about holding her close. It was about savoring our connection and the way our time together stitched our intimacy tighter and tighter, strengthening our bond.

Yet... her brother had been skeptical for a reason when I told him we were seeing each other. I preferred to keep my distance in relationships. As much as I loved my mother and my siblings and our close-knit family, we carried secrets and baggage, which often bounced off each other. It wasn't just Jake's death or his abuse at the hands of our grandfather. It was our father dying when we were young. McKenna was just a toddler and barely remembered him. It felt like so long ago. Losing him had changed our lives irrevocably.

My mother's grief had been a palpable weight in the house. Our parents had truly loved each other. I would never know whether our grandfather had abused our father. My mother said they had a tense relationship, but she wasn't aware of any physical or sexual abuse. We all wondered about it after things came to light about Jake.

A lesson meted out to me at a young age had been that losing someone you loved was painful, made worse when someone you should trust was abusive. While I hadn't been the target of my grandfather's abuse, beyond him being verbally gruff and intimidating with occasional slaps and strikes, I knew what he did to Jake. I'd seen him slap Jake so hard that Jake's head whipped back with such force his ears were ringing hours later.

In unconscious defense, I'd taught myself to keep my emotions quiet. Even though I knew I loved Haven, I'd kept a part of myself tucked away. If I wanted to make this work with Haven, I had to let myself be vulnerable in a way that hadn't been safe for me before.

She shifted in her sleep, letting out a soft sound. It felt as if the sound slung a silk lasso around my heart, cinching it tighter to her. I slid my hand up her back, sifting my fingers through her soft and fine curls. She often fretted that they were too messy, but I loved them. Their wildness was so much of her. Even when she was guarded, Haven's heart was apparent—her kindness, her sharp wit, and the edge of her loyalty ran deep. That loyalty was how I understood why she'd been hurt by her ex before and why she reacted so swiftly and protectively when she thought I'd hidden a massive secret from her.

It stung a little that she thought I could've ignored my son like that if I had one. I was already worrying over how to ensure Cathy didn't try to keep Matthew from us, and he was my nephew, not my son.

I took a deep breath, letting it out as I rolled my head to the side to look out the windows. The bedroom was at the back of the house with a view of the town harbor. The moon hung low in the sky, almost full and casting a pearly shimmer across the water. I fell asleep a few minutes later, feeling at peace for the first time in too long.

My sense of peace shattered the following morning. Haven had risen early, as usual, to go open Spill the Beans Café. I had walked down there with her, savoring the fresh, early spring air and the way the streets of downtown Fireweed Harbor were quiet and still. An eagle had called in the early morning with a raven taunting it.

Haven had made me coffee. I felt gratified at the pink flush on her cheeks when I kissed her goodbye before I left to go to the office.

A mere hour later, I was trying my damnedest to keep my cool. Our attorney had scheduled a meeting with Cathy and her attorney. When I asked where Matthew was, she'd looked over and said, "Not here."

I could handle her being snippy, but my mother was beside herself. She believed Matthew was her grandson, and she wanted to get to know him. Colin had told me to keep my mouth shut, and I was trying.

Colin's sharp gaze flicked from Cathy to her attorney. "Here's the thing. This all started because your client demanded child support from Rhys Cannon.

He's not the father. I think it's apparent why your client insisted the more in-depth paternity test was unnecessary. Had we done that, she may have been able to convince everyone that Matthew was Rhys's son. He's very likely Matthew's uncle, which means your client needs to come clean about who else in the family she had a relationship with. There are six brothers to choose from. We suspect the father is the deceased Jacob Cannon Jr. Now, either we set up a parade of DNA tests or your client can be honest. The family has already offered to cover child support and costs. Clara Cannon"—he gestured to my mother sitting beside me, her features drawn tight with tension—"would like a relationship with her grandson."

Cathy's attorney shifted in his chair. "This, I'm sure you'll agree, is a formidable family for my client to be going up against."

"Up against what?" My tone was icy cold and low. "I didn't even know my alleged son existed. He is ten years old. Now, to act like she's being attacked is complete bullshit. There's nothing wrong with us wanting a relationship with our brother's son." I looked toward Cathy. "I'm not sure what game you're playing here, but let's figure this out fast. If money is the issue, we've already made it clear we will provide the money even though Jake is dead, and we owe you nothing."

I felt my mother almost imperceptibly flinch at my words. I wanted to apologize to her, but I was too furious to focus.

Cathy straightened in her chair, her eyes a little wide. "I honestly didn't know which one of you was the father. I have not had a relationship with anyone else in the family." She looked offended that we'd even suggested it. I didn't give a flying fuck that she'd seen fit to be involved with both Jake and me at the same time. We'd been young. I was pissed off because I didn't know what she was after.

Holding her gaze, I replied, "We appreciate your honesty. What exactly did you want if it wasn't money?"

"I wanted my son to have a relationship with his father. Clearly, that's not possible. I thought it was you. I really did."

I wasn't sure I believed Cathy on that count, but it didn't really matter now, so I simply nodded. "Well, he's not my son. He's my nephew. As we have already stated, we're happy to provide financial support toward his care. All of that to say, we would also like the opportunity to build a relationship with him."

Cathy glanced from me to her attorney to my mother and back to me. She carefully guarded her expression. It had been over ten years since I'd seen her, but she was different. Back then, she'd been a party girl in college. Not too wild and rather practical about what she wanted. I knew from our attorney's detective work that she worked in marketing in San Francisco now.

"I'm not opposed to that," she said carefully.

I glanced at my mother. Her hands were resting on the table, laced together. Her fingers tightened. This entire situation had torn open the lingering wounds from my brother's death. His death had been painful for all of us.

"I would hope that since you're seeking child support, you would've expected the family to want a relationship. You told no one about him. To try to play the victim is disingenuous," I replied.

The corners of Cathy's mouth tightened, and she

lifted her chin slightly, a subtle flush on her cheeks. I sensed she hadn't been prepared to be confronted.

"I'm not trying to play the victim," she finally said.

"When can we meet him?" I cut through the dance of this conversation to the heart of the matter.

"Tomorrow, if you'd like. Where shall we meet?"

"At our offices." My mother and I had discussed this. She had originally proposed the house, but I still didn't trust Cathy's motives and preferred to start on more neutral territory.

Her attorney interjected, "We'd like to settle the terms of the child support first."

"It's technically not child support," Colin replied. "Jake Cannon is deceased. I suppose you could call this a simple agreement to provide survivor's benefits."

Cathy's eyes widened as she swallowed. I looked straight at her. "You said the relationship was important to you. While Jake isn't here to form that relationship, the rest of the family is."

We made arrangements and confirmed a meeting time at our family's offices the following day. Cathy reportedly had plans to leave in the next few weeks, although she hadn't confirmed travel dates.

After Cathy walked out with Colin and the other attorney conferring in the reception area, I turned to my mother. "How are you?" I asked quietly.

She finally unlaced her fingers and slid her palms down her slacks before angling her chair to face me. "I'm okay. Something feels off about this."

"Agreed. Regardless of her motives, the worst would be that she wants money. She'll get money."

My mother pressed her lips together before letting out a sharp sigh. "I don't like being so casual about it. Other people in this situation wouldn't be able to just toss money at it."

No one in my family felt particularly comfortable with our family's wealth. Be that as it may, the situation was what it was.

I held her gaze and shrugged. "I know. It's okay. We can provide support of some kind. Not a lump sum, just funds that go to his care. We can set up a trust, one that will transfer to him when he's an adult and be managed. That way, he's cared for in college and so on. Depending on how things turn out, we can consider whether he works for the family later. We have years before we have to sort that out."

My mother's eyes met mine. "I miss Jake," she said simply.

"We all do."

Moments later, I left, immediately walking toward Spill the Beans Café. I knew Haven was working, so we wouldn't be able to talk about this, but I needed to see her.

Main Street was starting to get busier in Fireweed Harbor. Although the cruise ships weren't coming every week now, they would be soon. Now that the snow was melting on the mountains and the days were getting warmer, tourists started crowding the streets. Already, the days were getting longer.

The sign for the café glinted as the sun angled across it, illuminating the shimmery pink lettering. Turning off the sidewalk, I smiled when I saw the bustling outdoor seating area under the covered porch. Customers were enjoying late-morning coffee and brunch.

I pushed through the doorway, my gaze arcing about the space when I didn't see Haven behind the counter. She was over in the corner collecting empty plates and mugs from a table. She wiped it down with one hand as she held the tray with dishes in the other.

I got in the back of the line, smiling at Phyllis when she looked up to see me. By the time I reached the front of the line, Haven was there with Phyllis taking the tray from her and saying, "I'll take this to the back. You take care of Rhys."

Haven bit her lips, pink tingeing her cheeks when she met my eyes.

"Hi," I said. My heart felt lighter just seeing her.

The urge to lean across the counter and kiss her was fierce, but I held back. Even before our recent breakup, she'd scolded me more than once for that. She smiled over at me, and my heart flipped in my chest. Fuck me. I had missed her. It was a relief not to be facing her icy coldness.

"Hey." Her voice was husky.

My need sharpened its claws. "How late are you working today?"

"Until four."

"Blake texted me. I was thinking we could go to the tasting tonight at the winery."

"I'd love that."

"Then we have a plan. Meanwhile, I'll take—"

My brother Kenan's voice came from over my shoulder. "I need coffee."

I glanced back, casting him a grin. "I do too."

He stopped beside me. "I know, so go ahead and order. Plus, I think you should get mine because you're taking too long."

I chuckled. "Happy to get yours."

Kenan glanced at Haven, waggling his eyebrows. "And how are you?"

She grinned. "Well, and yourself?"

"I'm freaking great. I'm headed out for some fishing."

"Oh, I love the first fishing trip of the season," she

replied. The bell above the door chimed behind us. "So what can I get you?"

We gave her our orders and stepped to the side as Phyllis came out to help Haven. Kenan glanced from me to Haven and back again. "It looks like you two might have sorted things out?"

Kenan and Adam were fraternal twins and the middle brothers. Kenan was older by a whopping three minutes and relished the opportunity to remind Adam of that time and again. He had my mother's coloring with dark brown hair and blue eyes. Adam shared my coloring. While Blake ran the winery, brewery, and restaurant, I headed up the headquarters for the corporation, and Adam was the CFO of everything, Kenan referred to himself as our "catch-all" because he did whatever we needed. He was flexible and easygoing. Wyatt and Griffin were my youngest brothers and also twins. They were just shy of two years younger than Adam and Kenan. They had eschewed working for the family because they both loved the outdoors and chased after adrenaline. They'd gone to hotshot firefighting training and landed on a crew up north for now.

Griffin was looking to score a spot on the hotshot crew here in Fireweed Harbor, although Wyatt stayed quiet on his plans. My mother still fretted and wanted both of them to come work for the company. Our only sister, McKenna, headed up our fundraising operations and public relations.

"I hope so," I said in reply to Kenan. "Speaking of the issue that interfered with Haven and me, Mom and I met with Cathy this morning. We're going to meet Matthew tomorrow."

"How is Mom?" Kenan asked, his gaze sobering.

I shrugged, rotating a hand in the air. "This whole

thing has brought up Jake and missing him. I think she's a little angry about the situation. Honestly, something just feels off." I let my breath out in a puff. "There's no doubt Matthew's related to us, but I don't trust Cathy's motives."

"I know exactly what's going on," Kenan said.

"You do?"

He nodded. "Dude, she wants you."

I eyed him skeptically, my brows hitching up. "Seriously? We're offering her money. If that's what she's after, she'll get it."

"She's going to get way more money if she hooks you," he pointed out.

I shook my head. "I don't believe it."

"Believe it. I saw the way she looked at you. She wants the cachet, but I don't know why she waited so long."

"I don't buy it," I said flatly.

"Mark my words. She's going to make a move."

Chapter Seventeen

HAVEN

That evening, I stood in my bedroom, eyeing myself in the mirror mounted on the back of the bathroom door. I fretted about my appearance. Rhys had texted me, pointing out that he considered tonight a date.

Something about this—trying again, him insisting he was going to court me, to woo me—had my nerves dancing.

For years, Fireweed Winery had weekly tastings. They were *events*. In addition to the yummy drinks, they used it as an opportunity for local artists to display their artwork. There were hors d'oeuvres for the tastings, and many stayed to have dinner in the restaurant.

While the Cannons certainly didn't need the money, these events bolstered the reputation they cultivated in the community. Supportive of the town, they often allowed non-profits to use the events to host fundraisers and the like. It was the place to see and be seen. Even though I had tried to avoid the gossip, I knew, without even the tiniest sliver of doubt, that my breakup with Rhys had run rampant like a brushfire.

With us going out tonight together, I wanted to look good. My skirt hugged my hips and flared around my knees, and I paired it with cowboy boots and a silky blouse with a little tie between my breasts.

I had just stepped into my boots when a knock sounded on the door. My belly fluttered, and my pulse kicked off. I'd actually missed the anticipation of seeing Rhys. It was a visceral experience. I nervously smoothed a hand over my hair as I approached the door. When I opened it, my belly swooped.

Rhys's intent gaze held mine for a beat before his eyes swept up and down my body. It felt as if he was taking my measure. Being the subject of Rhys's undivided attention felt much too good.

His lips kicked up at one corner when his eyes met mine again. He stepped closer, lifting a hand and palming my cheek as he dipped his head, murmuring, "Nice to see you, sweetness."

When his lips brushed over mine, it felt as if a hot flame raced through me. When he straightened, I took a quick breath. "Nice to see you."

His hand fell away from my cheek, and he reached for one of mine, curling his warm grip around it. "I don't really want to go anywhere," he said with a sheepish grin.

I didn't, either. I bit my bottom lip before releasing it as I replied, "We could stay in."

He lifted my hand, turning it over in his and dropping a kiss in the center of my palm. It felt like a hot pebble, sending ripples of heat radiating outward.

"We could, but I told Blake we were coming. And I promised to woo you."

Anticipation fizzed through me like bubbly champagne. My entire body celebrated, cheering at his presence and the way I felt when I was with him.

"Well, then we'd better go. I don't want to let Blake down," I teased lightly.

Rhys chuckled, lowering my hand but holding it firmly in his. "Are you ready to go?"

"Let me get my jacket." I looked down at our entwined hands. "I need my hand," I added regretfully.

He released it, and I snagged my jacket off the hook by the door and lifted my keys and wallet to tuck them in my pocket.

"Dinner is on me. You don't need your wallet," he commented.

I looked up at him. "Maybe so, but what if they ID me?"

His low chuckle sent a hot shiver over the surface of my skin.

"Are we walking or driving?"

Rhys glanced down as we stepped through the doorway. I turned to close it and double-check that it automatically locked.

"I thought we'd drive. It's still a little chilly out."

He tapped his key fob as we approached his black SUV. He drove a nice vehicle, but it was very practical. Four-wheel drive was a must in the winters of Alaska. Between the long winters and being tucked in the foothills of the mountains, it wasn't a wise proposition to try to go through winter without the option of four-wheel drive.

"This is the shortest drive ever," I said.

He grinned down at me. "It's at least a mile." He held the door for me, gesturing to the passenger seat.

"Wow, you're going all out," I teased.

"I usually hold the door for you."

"True." One of my feet was still on the edge of the

inside of the door when he placed a palm on my knee. His touch was warm.

"Wait."

I turned to look at him, and he leaned forward, sliding his palm over my knee, just under the edge of my skirt. My core clenched. Sweet hell. *This* man.

His intent silver-smoke gaze held mine, and my belly fluttered. "I meant what I said."

"What's that?" I rasped.

"We're going to get it right this time. We're going to take it slow."

My pulse galloped along, careening out of control, and my breath came in shallow pants. "Haven't we already skipped a few steps?" I managed to ask, trying to tease because I was nervous.

"Maybe so. We can't go backward, but we can build a stronger foundation this time."

"Okay," I whispered just before he dipped his head and brushed his lips over mine.

He teased his lips over mine in a slow, gentle kiss, barely letting his tongue tangle with mine.

When he drew back, I leaned forward, near desperate for more. His eyes darkened as he held my gaze, whispering gruffly, "More. Later."

Rhys made sure I'd buckled in before closing the door. I sat in the passenger seat, arousal slick between my thighs as we drove the short distance to Fireweed Winery.

He parked in the back of their main offices, next to the winery. He looked over at me, reaching his palm across the console to slide along my thigh.

I glanced over, instantly caught in his gaze, the look there sending a shower of sparks through me and heat pooling in my belly. He slid his palm up my thigh, teasing his fingers over the damp silk between my thighs. I bit my lip, letting out a whimper when he slid one finger under the edge of the elastic and teased it into my dripping wet folds.

"Just checking," he whispered.

A moan escaped when he drew his finger out.

I nearly combusted on the spot when he lifted it to his mouth and sucked my arousal off.

Chapter Eighteen
RHYS

I walked into the winery with Haven's hand held firmly in mine. My body was taut with need. I'd miscalculated. I'd wanted to tease her to distraction. While I hoped I'd succeeded, I'd left myself deeply aroused. I was willing the need beating with two fists on the door in my body to abate.

I was relieved when I heard my mother's voice. Not because I wanted to see my mother specifically at this moment but because her voice instantly knocked my body back to sanity.

I turned, seeing her approaching from the back hallway that led into the private area of the building. She smiled when she saw Haven. "Hi, dear," she murmured as she stopped in front of us, reaching over and lightly squeezing Haven's shoulder. As her hand fell away, she added, "You look lovely, as always."

Haven smiled. "It's nice to see you, Clara. You look great, as always."

My mother shrugged. "I try. Tonight is a busy one." She looked around the room.

My gaze arced about the space. "In addition to the

tasting, they have the quarterly show from Midnight
Sun Arts."

That was a local gallery that had locations scattered about Alaska. They'd opened one in Fireweed
Harbor, and they coordinated with our winery for
events. It was a mutually beneficial relationship where
they showed off local artists and brought new
customers to our restaurant.

"Well, it's good to see you both," my mother said.
"I'm going to make the rounds."

"Good to see you, Mom." I leaned over and
pressed a kiss on her cheek. She gave a little wave as
she began to weave her way through the crowd

"Where should we start?" I asked, glancing down
at Haven.

"I'm in the mood for a mead or wine."

While we had a regular production schedule for
wine, beer, and mead production, we had seasonal
flavors and annual limited runs. It was a way to keep
things fresh.

"According to Blake," I murmured as we began
making our way toward the bar at the back, "there's a
delicious new gooseberry wine. I haven't tried it yet,
though, so I can't vouch for it."

Haven smiled up at me when we stopped at the
corner of the bar. "I can honestly say I've never tasted
anything here that wasn't delicious. Even the beer is
good, and you know I'm not a huge beer fan."

I chuckled. "I'm glad we make wine and mead."

Blake caught my eyes from where he stood behind
the bar, filling a pint glass for a customer. "Be right
over," he mouthed.

I nodded and glanced around the space. Blake had
been renovating this entire area. He'd started in the
back by modernizing all of our brewing equipment,

which had been a significant investment. It had already paid off with substantially increased earnings in the past two years. Over this past winter, while business was quieter without the cruise ships, he'd renovated the public-facing areas himself. We'd all pitched in to help get it done faster, but he had done much of the work himself. Maybe our family had moved up in the world from when we started this place, but we were still very hands-on with the business.

Blake had kept the original bar. He had sanded down the wide wooden slab and refinished it to make the wood grain visible. It gleamed under the lights from above. Removing the low ceiling had exposed the old wooden beams. New lighting fixtures hanging from the ceiling in small glass globes cast a pleasant atmosphere.

The side windows offered a view of the harbor, while the front windows offered a view of Main Street. Round tables, wooden to match the bar, were scattered about the space. The seating area for the restaurant was through a large archway. Blake had eschewed hardwood flooring in that area, insisting he wanted people to enjoy a quiet meal. According to him, we didn't need the "false atmosphere" of loud flooring creating more noise. As it was, the restaurant was always busy. He kept the hardwood flooring where we had the tastings and bar seating because the risk of spills in this area was greater.

David, the restaurant's main chef, and manager, had a lot of input into the planning. He'd insisted we expand on one side to add a stage for occasional local bands. He wanted this to become a destination for music as well as wine and beer.

I knew we could do it. Blake had plenty of cash flow to work with and was motivated. He didn't want to ride the coattails of the established success and hoped to take things up a notch for the business.

Haven's voice reached me. "This place looks really good. Blake has done a fantastic job."

I smiled down at her. "Agreed."

"You'd better agree," Blake teased as he stopped in front of us, hearing Haven's comment.

"I'd like to take some credit," I teased in return, smoothing my hand over the bar. "I helped sand this."

"That you did." My brother grinned. "What do you want to try tonight?"

"Rhys says there's a new gooseberry wine and a limited run of wild blackberry mead. I'd like to try both."

Blake charged a fee for everyone coming in, so they got one free glass of whatever they wanted to try, and then after that, they had to pay. It worked out well enough because almost everyone got more, and plenty of people stayed for dinner in the restaurant.

I slid my credit card across the counter to Blake. "For our fees tonight."

"You know you don't have to pay."

"I'm paying. It's better for business."

Blake shrugged and quickly ran my card through his handheld reader. "Try the gooseberry wine first and then the mead," he said to Haven. "What about you?" He looked toward me.

"I'll try the new porter."

I'd already scanned the handwritten chalkboard with a list for this week's tasting. A few minutes later, he'd served both of us and had whisked away to attend to others.

Haven lifted her gooseberry wine and took a sip, closing her eyes as she swallowed. When she opened them, she smiled. "That is tasty. I've never had goose-berry wine, so I wasn't sure what to expect."

Blake handed a customer a glass and paused in front of us, waggling his eyebrows. "Well?"

"I love it," Haven said with a wide smile.

His sharp gaze shifted to me. "Excellent porter." I took another swallow.

"Are you two staying for dinner?"

"Definitely. This is a date," I replied.

"Emphasis on *date*," Blake teased.

Someone called my brother's name, and he flashed us a quick grin before spinning away. "Enjoy dinner. The steak special is really good," he tossed over his shoulder.

Haven took my hand after we finished our drinks. "Let's walk around and look at the artwork before we go into the restaurant."

We began to move slowly through the crowd. "It is really busy," she commented. "Busier than usual."

"Well, we've had two cruise ships this week. That means summer is officially here, even if the calendar doesn't say so."

She smiled up at me. "It's almost May."

"Rhys and Haven," a woman's voice said.

I knew that voice very well. Aside from Hazel and Phyllis at Spill the Beans Café, only one other person basically served as the town's circuit center. In the case of Hazel and Phyllis, while they were both very well informed, they also had location and coffee on their side. In the case of Mimi Smith, no one really knew how old she was, but she knew all. She had been born and raised in Fireweed Harbor and somehow knew everyone and every detail.

I turned, smiling blandly. "Hi, Mimi."

Her gaze dipped down to where my fingers were

laced with Haven's. Those piercing blue eyes lifted to mine again. Despite her weathered face and such a slight build that a hard gust of wind might blow her away, Mimi nearly vibrated with vitality. She was sharp, intelligent, and had a sly sense of humor. You wanted to stay on her good side, and she wouldn't hesitate to let you know if you didn't.

"I see you two are finally back together," she said, nodding firmly as if in agreement with the state of our relationship.

When I glanced at Haven, her cheeks were pink, but she chuckled. "We are."

I squeezed her hand.

Mimi pursed her lips, her gaze arcing about the crowded room before landing back on us. "You're a smart man."

"I hope so," I said, meaning it.

"Well, I'm sure you know that. In spite of your family's finances, I always liked you. I'm not inclined to like people who have too much money. But life has thrown other difficulties your way." Her gaze softened slightly, and I knew she was referring to Jake. I imagined she also knew the full story of our grandfather's actions. "I never liked Clint. Asshole," she said pointedly.

Haven made a choking sound. I shrugged when I glanced her way. "That's an accurate description." I looked back toward Mimi.

"I hope you can steer the ship on this other news," she added.

Comments like this were why you had to brace yourself when encountering Mimi. No topic was off-limits for her. I knew she was referring to Cathy, and I had no doubt that she already knew I was not the father.

She clucked, shaking her head. "Never stop being a good man." She looked at Haven. "And you're scrappy. You came back broke. I know you're getting your business going again, but I don't want you to leave the café. I like seeing you there every day."

Haven's eyes widened. "It's always good to see you there, Mimi."

"Ha! I doubt that, but feel free to bullshit me."

Haven burst out laughing. "I mean it! I have to prepare for what you may not be afraid to talk about, but I can handle it."

"I know you can." Mimi patted her on the shoulder. "Now, good luck."

With that, she was off.

"Good luck with what?" Haven asked as she glanced up at me.

"Hi, Rhys," a voice said smoothly from my side before I could reply to Haven.

I instantly knew why Mimi had wished us good luck. I almost let out a groan of frustration, but I took a breath, pasting the blandest smile I could on my face as I turned to see Cathy stopping beside me.

"Hi, Cathy," I said politely. "Have you met my girlfriend, Haven?"

I could feel Haven's tension. Her hand tightened incrementally in mine, and her shoulders stiffened slightly.

Cathy studied Haven for a moment before she nodded, just the littlest bit. Just enough to seem snooty, which put me off. "I think I've seen you before."

"Probably at Spill the Beans Café. I think you came in the other day," Haven said.

"Mmm. That must be it." Cathy glanced at me.

Her look was hopeful, but I had no idea what she was expecting.

"Yes?" I prompted.

"I was hoping we could talk," she said, leaning closer as if imparting something private.

Chapter Nineteen

HAVEN

I told myself I shouldn't feel threatened by Cathy. It didn't matter if she looked like a model. It didn't matter if she was conventionally beautiful and thin and willowy.

Rhys's hand held mine, and I could sense his frustration. "Anything we need to talk about, you can discuss in front of Haven," he finally said, his tone pointed.

Cathy's pretty blue eyes slid to mine, calculating and assessing. "I would like to speak privately. Obviously, you can choose to discuss whatever you want with her, but—"

Rhys took a quick breath. "Cathy, what do you need to talk about?"

"Your family wants a relationship with my son—" She began.

He cut right in, his tone icy cold. "Yes, Matthew is your son. He's also Jake's son and my nephew, and you chose to hide that information from us for his entire life. I would like to think you're not out for the money, but it sure seems like it. Lucky for you, we're willing to pay even though it won't be directly to you."

Two red splotches appeared on Cathy's cheeks, and she looked flustered. Her hand tightened around the small handheld clutch she held in front of her waist. "I understand why it might seem like that," she finally said. "I'll just repeat that I'd like to speak with you privately at some point." She cast me what could only be described as a glare. "You can let me know when that works for *you*."

I knew I was being baited into this, but I didn't want to drag it out. I gestured toward Cathy, saying to Rhys, "I thought I saw Tessa. I'll go find her and check in." I looked at Cathy. "You can chat while I'm gone."

Rhys glanced down. "Haven—" He began.

I tugged my hand free of his. "Just have the conversation. I'll come find you if I don't see you in a few minutes."

Not giving him a chance to reply, I slipped away. Conveniently, a server passed by with a tray full of wine glasses. He paused beside me. "Is that the gooseberry wine?" I asked, leaning close.

He nodded. "Help yourself." He held out the small piece of paper to mark my account for the bar.

After lifting one of the smaller glasses, I filled out my name for the bar tab. "Thank you."

I took a fortifying swallow before scanning the room. I forced my gaze to slide quickly past Rhys and Cathy. The lines of tension on his face were evident even from here. While he was trying to hold himself away, she was leaning close and placing her hand on his forearm. I was starting to get the feeling Cathy was after more than money.

A few minutes later, I found Tessa. "Hey, you!" She gave me a side hug, careful to keep her glass of wine out of the way. "Are you here with Rhys?" she asked after she stepped back.

I nodded before taking another swallow of my wine, about to finish off the whole glass. "He's talking with Cathy. She wanted a private conversation."

Tessa rolled her eyes. "I ran into Blake the other day. He was at the store when I was there getting supplies for class." Tessa taught first grade at the local elementary school. "He was catching me up on the whole situation. He thinks she's after Rhys."

I gritted my teeth. "I think Blake might be right."

"Blake says there's no chance Rhys wants anything to do with her. The whole family is pissed off that she hid Jake's son from them for all these years."

"I can't say I blame them. I remember what it was like for them when Jake died. It was so sad. They were devastated when it happened."

"Heartbreaking," Tessa agreed.

Just then, I felt Rhys's presence before he reached me. I glanced over my shoulder to see him approaching from the side. He stepped around a couple and then stopped beside me, sliding his arm around my waist. "There you are."

Tessa smiled at us. "Here she is. How long has it been?"

Rhys chuckled. "Five minutes tops." He glanced down at me. "I'm going to run to the restroom. I thought we could grab a table after that."

"Sounds like a plan. I'll wait right here."

He brushed a kiss on my cheek. I nearly shuddered at the hot shiver that raced through me. I watched as he threaded through the crowd toward the restrooms on the side of the room. When I looked back at Tessa, my cheeks were burning.

She gave an exaggerated brow waggle. "I don't

think you need to worry about Rhys wanting anyone other than you. Aside from the scoop on Cathy, Blake told me Rhys missed you like crazy, and he's swearing up and down he'll get it right this time. That man is totally into you." Her gaze softened. "And you deserve it."

I let out a little sigh. "No more so than you do." I gave her a friendly nudge with my elbow.

Tessa had just gotten out of a sticky divorce. She was swearing on anything to be sworn on that she would never fall in love again.

"I'm good. I'm going to enjoy being single for the rest of my life. In fact, I did laundry the other day just because it was just my laundry. It was one of those mini loads. I set it on the short cycle, and it was amazing."

"You might change your mind." I shrugged. "I'm just glad you're on the other side of that."

"No shit. My marriage was an epic disaster. Anyway, before your hot man crush gets back and sweeps you off your feet for dinner, can I propose we meet for brunch this weekend?"

"Yes! Sunday. I'm not working at the coffee shop. Let's plan on it."

Rhys reappeared, and we headed in to dinner. As soon as he sat down, he announced, "Cathy says she plans to stay in town for a month or more."

Chapter Twenty

RHYS

I had a sinking feeling that Blake might be right about Cathy. It didn't change a thing for me, except for being a nuisance. She'd been touchy-feely with me when we'd been talking, a little arm brush here and there, a tad too familiar. I didn't want to dwell on Cathy, though.

Haven set down her fork, lifting her napkin and dabbing at her mouth before she laid it on the table. "That was so good."

She'd gotten a seared salmon steak with a lemon tarragon sauce. I'd gotten the steak Blake had recommended. We'd tasted bites from each other's plates.

She cocked her head to the side, studying me before commenting, "You're thinking."

"I'm always thinking," I teased lightly.

"Maybe, but you look worried. You look..." She paused, drumming her fingertips on the table. "Worried and annoyed, maybe?"

I hesitated. I didn't want to give her a reason to worry about anything because there was *nothing* to worry about with Cathy. But I also knew with Cathy announcing her plans to stay in town for a little while that she would be around. I didn't precisely trust Cathy.

I took a quick breath. "Like I said, Cathy told me she's planning to stay in town for a little while."

Haven's brows hitched up as she nodded.

"She says she wants to give us time to get to know Matthew. I'll be honest, I don't trust the situation. She was initially hesitant about us getting to know him after it was clear he was not my son. Of course, my mom wants to get to know him, and so do the rest of us."

"You haven't said, but do you think she really thought he was yours?"

"She said as much at the meeting."

"Do you think something else is going on?"

I shrugged because I didn't genuinely know. "Hard to say. She's getting money. If that's what she's after, we're giving her exactly what she wants."

"I suppose you should just wait and see. I know this is probably bringing up a lot about Jake."

"It is."

Haven studied me quietly for another moment. "Do you want to talk about it?"

I shook my head. "Not right now. Jake's death will always be a sore spot for my family. There's not a whole lot to say about it other than that."

She reached across the table, where my hand was resting, and laced her fingers through mine. "I know. I'm sorry."

"Thank you." My voice came out gruff, and I cleared my throat.

Someone laughed at a table nearby, and our server appeared, glancing back and forth between us. "Are you finished eating?"

Haven smiled up at him. "Yes. Everything was great."

He collected our plates, asking, "Dessert?"

Haven caught my eyes. "What do you think?"

"I think we should share that chocolate mousse."

"I can vouch for it," the server offered with a quick smile. "It's very good."

"Let's share it," Haven said with a grin.

My sister's voice sounded from behind me, and I glanced over my shoulder to see her approaching our table. She stopped beside us, her smile warm. "Well, hello, lovebirds," she said.

I cast her a dry look.

"Lovebirds?" Haven teased as she looked up at McKenna.

"Rhys is in love with you, so you're lovebirds. It's so good to see you back together." McKenna's hand landed on my shoulder and she squeezed lightly before it fell away. "How was dinner?"

"Excellent," Haven said. "My only complaint here is that they rotate the specials. I know every place does that, but they're always so good. I'd like them to keep everything on the menu."

McKenna chuckled. "Agreed. We'll have to tell David."

"Did you taste the gooseberry wine?" I asked.

"I did. Very good. Anyway, I just wanted to say hello. I meant to get here sooner, but work was busy."

McKenna handled public relations for our corporation and liked to keep it personal. She had a small department and kept on top of everything.

"It's always busy," I replied.

My sister rolled her eyes. "True story. Good to see you both."

I bit back the urge to point out that I saw her almost every day. But I knew she was commenting on Haven and me being back together, so I didn't. She asked Haven about her online business. McKenna was planning to hire Haven to create some cards for an event for our foundation. I was relieved for the distraction because I really didn't want to dwell on any news about Cathy.

After McKenna departed, Haven smiled over at me. "I think she's happy we're having dinner."

"She's thrilled," I said dryly. "I'm surprised she didn't cheer for us."

Haven was quiet for a beat before lifting her glass of water and taking a swallow.

"Have you heard from Deacon recently?" I asked.

"We haven't talked in a week or so. He told me I shouldn't have made assumptions so quickly around the child support paperwork."

I laughed softly. "Well, he is my best friend. I would hope so."

When she bit her bottom lip and her cheeks tinged pink, I wanted to lean across the table and kiss her. That was the thing with Haven—every moment was foreplay.

Our dessert arrived, and within moments, I decided watching Haven eat chocolate mousse was a special form of torture.

She lifted the spoon, her lips closing around it as she dragged it out slowly, murmuring, "Mmmmm." When she drew it away, she slid her tongue along her bottom lip and closed her eyes. "So good," she enthused when she opened them.

It *was* good, but now I just wanted to finish and get out of here.

We were seated in a small booth, tucked into a corner. I slid around the curved seat beside her, placing my palm on her knee. "Why don't you just eat all of it?"

She peered up at me. "I can't finish this, or I'll be way too full."

I took a bite, sliding my hand up her thigh under the hem of her skirt.

"One more bite," I murmured as I used my other hand to lift the spoon for her.

Haven's lips closed around the spoon. She let out a little moan, her eyes on mine the whole time. Reflexively, my fingers pressed into the soft give of her thigh. She shifted her legs, and I couldn't resist, sliding my palm up to cup her mound

She blinked. "Rhys!" she whispered fiercely.

"Nobody can see." I teased my fingers over the damp silk.

I hadn't forgotten the taste of her from earlier, hours ago now, when I had teased her in the car before we came in.

"Let's go," I whispered gruffly, reluctantly drawing my hand away.

I had already sent the server off with my credit card, and he conveniently returned just then. I added a generous tip before we left.

With her hand firmly in mine, we walked through the restaurant and out the back entrance.

Need was cracking its whip behind me. Even the parking lot was crowded with groups of people walking in and others leaving. As we crossed to the parking area behind the main offices for Fireweed Industries, I made a quick decision. "Let's go to my office."

Haven came to a stop, and I looked down. "Now?" she squeaked.

"Right now."

Her lips curled at the corner as she whispered, "Okay."

I keyed in the combination to the back entrance and forced myself to wait, making sure the door locked automatically behind us. I took her hand and tugged her up the stairs. The offices were dark, and the carpeted floor muted our footsteps. We made it up to the second floor, where my office was. We moved down the hallway, out of sight of the windows that looked over Main Street.

I turned her against the wall, placing my palms on either side of her shoulders as I looked down at her. "I need you."

Her eyes held mine as she nodded once. I claimed her mouth in a kiss, and her tongue met mine, stroke for stroke. Her palm pressed against my chest, and my heart lunged toward it. After a month of missing her fiercely, I felt reckless, rushed, and near frantic for her.

I ran my hand down her side, pausing briefly to cup her breast and drag my thumb roughly over her nipple. Hooking my fingers on the hem of her skirt, I dragged it up, bringing my hand right back to where it had been earlier. I didn't wait before shoving her panties to the side and delving my fingers into her slippery wet folds.

I broke free from our kiss, staring into her dark, passion-hazed gaze as I sank two fingers into her, knuckle-deep. Her hips bucked into my touch.

"Fuck, Haven, you're so wet," I bit out.

Her head thumped against the wall. "Rhys... I... need..."

Forcing myself to break away, I grabbed her hand and tugged her another few steps down the hallway into my office. I kicked the door shut behind us. A moment later, we were in front of my desk. I was rushed as I yanked her panties down. By some miracle, I got them off without getting them tangled in her boots. I lifted her up onto my desk, shoving her skirt up around her hips. The only light came from the security light in the corner, low and dim.

"Spread your knees, sweetness."

She complied instantly. The sight of her pussy bared for me—slick, swollen, and pink from her arousal—sent a shot of blood straight to my groin. I was already aching with need for her.

She reached between her thighs, almost as if she couldn't help herself, teasing her fingers through her wet folds.

"Fuck me," I groaned.

Haven held my gaze. "Please do," she rasped.

She moved her hand away, reaching toward me, deftly unbuttoning and unzipping my jeans. Her palm slid into my briefs, and she shoved my jeans and boxers down around my hips. My cock sprang free. I growled when she curled her palm around it, her touch silky smooth.

"Baby, I need to taste you," I whispered through gritted teeth.

She looked up at me. I reached down, tugging her hips closer to the edge of the desk before leaning down and bringing my mouth to her sex. She tasted salty, tangy, and a little sweet. I savored the way her hips bucked against my mouth and the sting on my scalp when one of her hands gripped my hair as she cried my name.

I knew how to bring her to the edge. Sinking my fingers inside her again, I pumped slowly as I swirled my tongue around her clit before sucking lightly. She shuddered against me, crying my name as she came against my mouth.

I waited until the ripples started to slow before drawing back and straightening. Her breath was coming in sharp pants. I couldn't wait any longer. I *needed* to be inside her.

Fisting my cock, I brought my mouth to hers and kissed her as I notched my crown at her entrance. I lifted my head, waiting until she said, "Please, Rhys."

I filled her slowly, inch by inch, watching as her lips parted. She let out a little whimper when I seated myself fully.

"Look at me, sweetness," I murmured when her lashes started to fall.

She looked up, staring into my eyes as I began to pump into her, savoring the feel of her silky, clenching sheath as I drove deep with each thrust. My release was right there, my balls tightening and lightning about to strike.

"Come for me, just once more."

Gripping her hip with one hand, I reached between us and instantly found her swollen clit, slippery from her arousal. Her eyes went wide before she cried out sharply and her pussy clenched around me.

I finally let go, and that lightning struck, sizzling through me in a fiery burst. I shuddered against her.

Chapter Twenty-One

HAVEN

Rhys held me close with one arm wrapped around my waist and the other sifting through my hair. I could feel the thundering beat of his heart against my chest as my own galloped along.

He'd just fucked me in his office. It felt dirty and intensely intimate.

God, I'd missed him so. It wasn't the sex and the orgasms, although those were incredible—it was how I felt with him. So close to him, so protected and cherished.

Rhys was solicitous after we untangled ourselves, helping me tidy my clothes. He paused at the door to his office before opening it, looking down at me. My belly flipped. Even though my body was sated, I knew it was only temporary. Emotional aftershocks of our intimacy reverberated through me as almost a visceral feeling.

"What?" I finally asked.

His shoulders rose with a breath, falling as he let it out. He held one of my hands and squeezed it gently before lifting my palm and brushing a kiss across the back of it.

"Nothing new," he murmured, bending low and dusting a kiss across my lips.

As we walked through the offices, it felt as if we were in a secret world of our own since no one else was there. Once we were in his SUV and he was driving the short distance home, he slid his gaze to mine briefly. "You've ruined my desk for me."

"Ruined?" I teased.

His chuckle was low and sent heat in a swirl through me. I had told myself I was going to be resolute and take things slow. When he parked in front of his house—the proximity to mine the very reason I'd ended up stumbling into this lust-fueled relationship with him—I looked over, studying his profile. The streetlight caught glints of dark gold in his hair. He had strong cheekbones, the lines delineated in the shadowed light. His nose was straight, almost perfectly so, and he had a strong, square jaw. I wanted to trail my fingertips along it. That was the problem with him. I always wanted more.

Even though I had told myself I wasn't going to let him spend the night, I did. I was the one who invited him in. He hesitated a little, saying, "We're going to take it slow."

I pointed out the obvious. "Taking it slow doesn't mean we can't sleep together. Considering what just took place in your office, that might be the least of our worries."

He chuckled and kissed me. After that, I slept curled up against his side, telling myself we would be okay this time.

Chapter Twenty-Two

HAVEN

One week later

"There you go," I said, sliding a tray of to go coffees across the counter.

The woman waiting stuffed a twenty-dollar bill in the tip jar. "Thank you!" She smiled over at me. "I know this order was complicated. I took this cruise with my friends, and we're having a blast, but three of them like really elaborate coffee drinks."

I grinned. "Well, I suppose there are worse things to worry about."

"Absolutely. It's my divorce cruise, and they've made it much better."

Since she smiled with her comment, I smiled again, waving as she left. Another cruise ship was in town, and we were slammed. By the time I got to the end of the line, my wrists were tired from working the espresso machine.

I shook my arms out, and Hazel smiled over at me.

"You can slow down the pace, you know," she said as she organized the baked goods display on the counter.

"It doesn't make less work," I returned.

She laughed softly, glancing around the café. While patrons occupied all the tables, the lunch rush was mostly over. The locals getting lunch were already seated and served, and we'd finally gotten through a solid hour of one customer after another coming in for coffee.

I started wiping down the espresso machine and the counters. Hazel finished transferring the afternoon selection of baked goods into the display case and glanced my way as she turned and rested her hips on the counter.

"How are things with Rhys?"

I almost laughed—not at her question but at myself. He was definitely wooing me. He'd taken me out to dinner four times in a single week. We'd spent all but two nights together. My restraint was a joke, although I suppose his was as well.

As my cheeks heated, Hazel's smirk was sly. "I guess it's going well."

My lips tugged into a smile. "I think so. I just don't want to screw it up this time."

"You didn't screw it up before."

"I think I kind of did. Things moved really fast. Against my better judgment, I fell for him. I'm still convinced he's out of my league."

Hazel studied me before rolling her eyes. "I don't agree."

"Of course, you don't agree," I retorted. "You're my protective boss."

"And I have eyes," she countered pointedly. "Rhys *is* handsome. And you're beautiful."

"But—" I began.

She held her palm up in the air, shaking her head sternly. "But what? You don't see yourself the way others do. You remember feeling awkward in high school and letting that define you. Most people feel awkward in high school. It's a hellish time." She visibly shuddered.

"Maybe so, but I've seen Cathy. She's the kind of woman I would expect Rhys to date. She's tall, blond, and classically beautiful."

"That's what I call average." Hazel's tone was dry.

"She's not average!"

"She's pretty boring as far as beautiful goes. You've got those gorgeous strawberry-blond curls, lovely eyes, and an actual figure. I once knew a guy. I was friends with him in college. Totally platonic," she said with a dismissive wave. "I was in love with my Ralph."

"Of course, you were," I interjected.

She smiled softly. "Anyway, my friend was a football player, kind of popular, probably like how you thought Rhys was when you were younger."

"Rhys *was* popular."

She waved dismissively again. "So what if he was? Not my point here. So I was friends with this guy because we had a couple of classes together. Really nice guy, and really smart too. Anyway, he had plenty of average beautiful women at his beck and call. He told me once that he felt like there was nothing to them. He wasn't even being mean about it. He meant nothing to hold on to emotionally. That it was all surface. I'm not bashing Cathy. She could be a perfectly nice woman and have a lot of depth to her. But you're intimidated by the surface, and that's not what anyone falls in love with."

I twisted my mouth to the side as I studied her.
"Well, no."

One of her brows arched up. "Did you fall in love
with Rhys because of his looks?"

"Oh no, but maybe in lust."

Hazel snorted. "I think you understand my point.
Maybe you're questioning yourself, but I understand
why getting those court papers made you draw back. It
was rational, under the circumstances. Rhys wasn't
known for being serious with anyone before you. Like
the rest of us, he was immature. He grew past that. I
can't tell you how things will go in the long run for you
two, but I can tell you that the way it starts is only one
part of the story. Ralph and I were head over heels at
first. At the time, I thought nothing could go wrong."
Her lips curled in a sad smile. "When I had my third
miscarriage, I wasn't sure we were going to make it.
We had more challenges after that. To this day, if he
came back from the dead, I would instantly be
annoyed with how loud he chewed."

I burst out laughing. Her eyes twinkled as she
grinned back at me. "It probably doesn't feel like it,
but it's better to have a challenge now that you need to
deal with and see how you get to the other side of it.
We all have reasons to distrust life and others. You
certainly have yours, as does Rhys. His family has been
through a lot. We can easily look at them as being
charmed. In some ways, they are, but in others, they
aren't. Sure they have money, but Jake drinking himself
to death was not the only shock for them. Their father
died when they were young, and their grandfather was
violent. He had a terrible temper. From the outside,
they all look so close, and they are, but tragedy tends
to draw people together."

The bell chimed on the door, and we both looked to see a cluster of tourists coming in with shopping bags dangling from their arms. Hazel caught my eyes once more. "I'm glad you're giving Rhys a chance. I have a good feeling."

Chapter Twenty-Three

RHYS

Blake slapped his palm against one of the large brewing tanks in the back, the sound a muted reverberation. "We're off to a good start for the spring. Numbers look great for wholesale orders." He turned, resting his hip against the tank.

"We're always off to a good start in the spring. This place did well before you took over, but you've taken it up a notch. I'm glad you're enjoying it," I replied.

"I love it," my brother said, his gaze sober. "Honestly, when I was younger and knew you were going to step into the CEO role, I was originally a little jealous, thinking I wanted to be in charge of everything." He let out a dry laugh. "Now, I have a lot more sense. You carry a lot on your shoulders."

I snorted. "That's one way to put it."

I understood Blake's point. Back when I thought Jake was going to lead the corporation, I'd experienced twinges of envy. But that wasn't how it played out. Some days, I'd give anything to handle something smaller, a side gig with less responsibility and low pressure.

I didn't have that choice. After Jake died, the feeling that I needed to fill his shoes and ease the pain of his death weighed on me. I'd never hesitated to step in. I did like my job, even if sometimes it was more than I wanted. I had a responsibility to my family, to the business, and to our community.

"Should we trade?" I teased.

Blake's eyes widened as he shook his head forcefully. "Hell, no. I actually love that I get to handle the winery and the brewery. Keeps me busy. People love me. It's beer, wine, and mead. It's not all fun and games, but..." He flashed a grin before letting out a breath. "Speaking of things I need to handle, I feel like I'm half-assing it every summer. The weekly tastings pretty much run themselves. I need to get more organized and..." He paused, studying me for a beat. "I'm planning to add more events."

"This is your baby. Whatever you think we should do, I trust your judgment."

"We're gonna have to start scouting for a new chef for the restaurant. David wants to slow down."

David had been the chef for the restaurant since my mom hired him twenty years ago. "Has he said anything official?"

"He's officially told me that he plans to cut back at some point. I don't think he wants to leave, but with his back and knee problems, it's tough for him to be on his feet that much. He's going to lead the search for a new chef."

"If tasting samples is part of the interview process, I'll help," I offered magnanimously.

Blake chuckled. "I'd love that." His gaze sobered. "How are things with Mom? I was over there the other day, and Cathy was there with Matthew."

"Good, I think. What do you think?"

Blake was quiet for a few beats, drumming his fingertips lightly against the tank behind him. "I'm glad to get to know our nephew, and I hope he wants to get to know us long-term. But I won't lie, it's weird. To him, we're strangers. Mom told me Cathy said she's only staying for a little while. I'm not sure we'll see much of Matthew after that." His eyes narrowed. "She make a move on you yet?"

Unfortunately, Cathy had. She'd stopped by my office, ostensibly just to sign off on some final paperwork. She *had* signed the paperwork, so it wasn't like that was total bullshit. But once again, there were too many light touches. Then she flat-out told me she had never stopped thinking about me.

I hadn't even replied to my brother, but Blake seemed to read my thoughts and shook his head slowly as he snorted. "Called it."

"Dude, I didn't even say anything."

"You're looking all uncomfortable."

I sighed. "Yeah. You and Kenan both saw this coming."

"I think you'll have to make it crystal clear to her that you aren't interested in that."

I ran a hand through my hair. "I don't want to make it a thing. I'd almost rather just ignore it."

"You can do that, but Cathy strikes me as the kind of person who needs a boundary set, a *really* clear boundary."

"I just want to focus on Haven, and I don't want this to be a problem."

"How are things with Haven?"

"Good, but they were good before."

"I know you're a little salty she reacted the way she did about that paperwork, but she's not crazy. You were never an asshole before, but you were also never known for being serious with anyone. You used to date people for maybe one to three weeks, tops. Nobody wants to think someone's hiding a kid from them. Not to mention, if Matthew had turned out to be your kid, then she had to be prepared to be a stepmom someday."

"We aren't ready for marriage," I muttered.

"Maybe not, but you said you love her, so you better start thinking about staying committed." My brother's eyes narrowed. "That makes you nervous."

"No, it doesn't," I protested, ignoring the sliver of uneasiness inside me.

He chuckled. "Sure, whatever you say."

Chapter Twenty-Four

RHYS

That evening, I was at my place. I looked through the kitchen window as I washed a few coffee mugs in the sink, then set them on the drying rack. My kitchen window looked directly into Haven's kitchen window. Our houses were mirrors of each other. Last summer, the small kitchen fire in Haven's house had brought me rushing over to her place one evening. That was when we ended up kissing for the first time.

I knew Haven's lease was coming up for renewal soon. I'd told myself I wasn't even going to ask our property manager about Haven's plans. Even contemplating that felt like I was getting ahead of myself. I was wondering solely because I was trying to sort out when I planned to build my own place. Staying here was temporary for me.

Haven had invited me over for pizza tonight, telling me I couldn't come over until after six because she needed to work on some graphic designs. I put the last mug in the dish rack and turned off the water. After I dried my hands, I glanced around.

My thoughts kept circling back to Blake's observation. I was restless after a month of missing Haven and finally getting her back. I craved losing myself in her.

Yet when Blake mentioned marriage, uncertainty, and anxiety tightened their screws in me. I loved Haven, but the idea of taking that next step sent panic unspooling inside me. I didn't understand it.

I ignored the feeling, ordering myself not to think too much about it. What I'd said to Blake was accurate. We weren't there. Before our recent breakup, we'd only been together since last summer.

We needed to build a stronger foundation. Right?

I felt satisfied with that train of thought, even nodding to myself.

My phone vibrated where it rested on the corner of the counter. Crossing over, I glanced down to see a text from Cathy.

Cathy: *Matthew is going to be with your mother for the evening. She's taking him to a kids' play theater group. I'd love to get together for dinner.*

I stared at her text, once again contemplating Blake's spot-on observations. I needed to set a boundary. As ridiculous as I thought it was, Cathy seemed to be making a play for me. Even when I'd been younger and with her in college, she hadn't held my attention for long. No one had. I could blame myself for being young, shallow, and not looking for much in relationships. Now, if I were honest, I wasn't interested in a woman like Cathy anymore.

Even if I wasn't attached to Haven and in love with her, Cathy and I had no chemistry. Beyond the lack of chemistry, I didn't see *any* way to recover from the fact that she'd hidden a child from our family for a decade. That secret was too big.

I decided being blunt with her was in order. I had

no interest in playing this game, so I needed to cut her off at the pass now.

Lifting my phone, I tapped my reply.

Me: *I'm not sure what you're after, but I'm not interested in dinner, lunch, or otherwise.*

Reconsidering my words, I deleted that immediately before hitting send. The line I walked at the moment was how to maintain the fragile connection my mother was building with Cathy to foster a relationship with Matthew and the rest of us.

I tried again, this time starting my reply in the notes app to avoid accidentally sending it before I was ready.

Me: *I'll have to pass. I have other plans with Haven.*

I reread that, nodding to myself before rolling my eyes. I was busy satisfying myself with my responses this morning. This made it clear Haven was my girlfriend and shouldn't offend Cathy.

I quickly pasted the text in. After I hit send, I glanced at the clock. Fifteen minutes until I could see Haven.

Chapter Twenty-Five

HAVEN

The following morning, when my alarm went off, I rolled over and tapped to turn it off on my phone. I instantly rolled back over, curling against Rhys's side. He was warm and all muscle-y.

I very much did *not* want to get out of bed. His arm curled around my shoulders, pulling me closer against him before his palm slid down my back, curving over the top of my bottom.

"Mmm," he murmured. "I love waking up with you." His voice was velvety soft around the edges.

I rested my head in the curve of his shoulder, my fingers trailing through the light dusting of hair on his chest. "I love waking up with you too," I whispered.

It was four-thirty in the morning, and I needed to be at Spill the Beans Café in an hour. Although the days were rapidly getting longer, sunrise was just teasing us right now. I lifted my head, peering out the window that looked out over the harbor. Where the mountains were visible in the distance on one side of the harbor, I could see the first glimmers of the sun's rays reaching into the sky.

I looked down at Rhys to find him watching me. "I don't want to get up," I announced.

His smile curved against his cheek. He pulled me down, bringing my mouth to his for a lazy, sensual kiss. By the time he drew back, liquid heat pooled low in my belly, and my pulse was skittering wildly. We stared at each other in the thin light of dawn. He squeezed my bottom before giving me a light spank.

"Get up, sweetness. It's time for a shower."

A short while later, I was leaning against the tiled wall in the shower with pleasure ricocheting through my body. Rhys had just had me against this very wall.

I sighed as I rolled my head back and forth against the tile. "No fair."

"What's not fair?" He caught my hand and pulled me under the water raining down from above.

"Now, I just want to go back to bed."

A sly glint entered his gaze. He turned the water from hot to cold for just a second.

"Rhys!"

"We both needed that." He turned the hot water back on.

"I might beg to differ on that." I rolled my eyes.

Although, his point turned out to be true. I was instantly alert. After we finished showering and got dressed, he glanced over. "Shall I walk you in?"

"This early? You don't have to."

"I like it. I'm an early riser as it is. I'll get a coffee and go to the office. I'm very productive when no one else is there."

A giddy sense of joy rose inside me, and I felt heat climb in my cheeks. We walked through the crisp spring morning to the café. I made him a coffee, and he left me with a lingering kiss.

I loved the quiet morning time at the café. We opened at six, and the half an hour between arriving and opening was my favorite time. I took the chairs off the tables, put the prepped pastries and muffins in the ovens, and sipped on my own coffee after heating up one of the pastries left over from the day before.

When my eyes landed on my business cards for With Love tucked beside the register with a few other local advertisements, I thought back to this time last year. Back then, I'd been living with my boyfriend. He had helped me get my online business up and running. I had started it while I was in college working at a coffee shop in Boston. I used to have fun getting the chalkboard menu ready every day there, making it artsy and putting lots of flair into it. My boss at the time had asked me to make wedding invitations for his daughter. He'd paid me well and even recommended I make my own business cards to leave them at the shop there. That was how it all started.

I did small batches of handmade selections and print runs for the more popular choices. It had started slow and gradually gotten busy enough to actually make money. My boyfriend had helped me set up the website. I had started to make enough money that I didn't have to work coffee shop jobs on the side. Unbeknownst to me, he'd been redirecting the money to his own bank account for enough months that I was close to broke by the time I figured it out. Then he was gone.

Feeling bitter and disillusioned, I'd taken what little money I had left and moved back home after my parents offered to help with my ticket home. They lived in Juneau now.

It had all worked out for the best. I'd missed Fireweed Harbor for years, and now I was home. What had started as a fling with Rhys had turned into so much more. Even during that bitter month when we'd broken up, I was still glad to be back in Fireweed Harbor. It was home. I had friends and people who had known me since I was a little girl. My business was starting to rebound as well.

I glanced at the clock and finished a bite of the spinach-and-cheese-stuffed pastry I had heated up before rounding the counter and turning on the lights that circled the windows. Moments after I turned the open sign at the door, McKenna came walking through.

Her smile was wide when she saw me. "Good morning!" she called.

"Good morning," I returned.

She stopped in front of the counter, resting her hands on it. Her eyes lifted to the chalkboard. "Ooh, I would love the salted caramel latte. I wish I could pretend to be more sophisticated and just get a straight espresso, but I love the sugary drinks."

"They're good. I like straight espresso, but I like the sweet stuff too. What size?"

"Whatever's medium."

I grabbed one of the medium-size cups with the Spill the Beans logo with pink lettering and spilled coffee beans underneath to begin prepping her coffee. "Anything to eat?" I asked as I tapped the button to start her coffee.

She perused the chalkboard again. "I would like a ham-and-cheese croissant and one of the cranberry-orange muffins to go. I need savory and sweet," she said as she smiled over at me.

"That's the way to start the day. I'll heat them for

you." I pulled them out of the case and turned to place them in the small oven.

As I was adding the syrup to her coffee, she startled me. "I want to hire you."

"Huh? For what?" Way to go with being professional.

McKenna was unfazed. "I don't know if you've heard, but Blake plans to add more events for the winery."

"I hadn't, but it makes sense."

"I'm always outsourcing promo materials for any of our public relations events. I know you mostly focus on wedding invitations and family events for what you do online, but we could hire you to be in charge of the artwork for all of the promo for his events and our public relations campaigns. What do you think? Is that in your wheelhouse? Or too far out of your zone?"

I stared at her before a big smile stretched across my face. "That is absolutely in my wheelhouse. My zone has been wedding invitations because that's how I started, but I've always been open to other projects. I love this!" I took a deep breath. "Are you sure? I mean, Fireweed Industries is big."

McKenna shrugged like it was totally no big deal that her family owned an international corporation. "Maybe so, but this part of our business isn't huge. I plan promotional campaigns every quarter. Blake will be planning a year in advance, so there will be plenty of lead time."

"Do I need to do samples for you?"

She shook her head. "I see your work all the time. The chalkboard here is a great sample. I've seen your wedding invitations as well."

"Oh, wow." I took a slow breath, trying not to

seem too excited. "How much work are we talking about?"

McKenna cocked her head to the side as she smiled. "We'll keep you busy. I don't think you'll need to keep the café job. The only thing we need to discuss is sorting out your fees."

I wanted to come across as casual—like it was no big thing that this could be a significant contract for my business—but I completely failed. I clasped my hands together, squeezing them tightly as I smiled over at her. "I'm so excited! Thank you for asking me." Just then, the timer on the small oven beeped, and I turned to remove her pastries and put them in a bag.

She beamed back at me. "You'll take our marketing to the next level. Anyway, I've gotta run." She lifted the coffee cup I'd slid across the counter and reached for the small paper bag with her pastries, handing over a twenty-dollar bill. "Keep the change. I'll text you."

Only moments after McKenna left, a cluster of tourists came in, keeping me busy. Hazel had arrived and came out front to refill the display case and help me out at the espresso machine. We had a pretty good rhythm and quickly got through the group.

Once we had a break, I glanced at Hazel. "Mind if I take a bathroom break?"

"As if you need to ask," she deadpanned, waving me away. "I have it covered."

While we had a staff bathroom in the back, the one up front was much closer, so I hurried over. After I took care of business, I washed my hands in the sink and splashed cold water on my face before dabbing it with a paper towel. I studied my reflection in the mirror for a moment. As usual, my curls had gotten the best of my ponytail. Several had escaped, one pointing out to the side and another one straight up above my forehead. I rolled my eyes and used the damp paper towel to smooth them back.

Just then, the door opened, and I reflexively glanced over, feeling an uneasy jolt when I saw Cathy walk in. She smiled over at me, everything about her seeming, well, classy and serene.

"Hi," she said.

Even her voice was smooth and melodic.

"Hi," I said, my voice coming out a little squeaky. Whenever I was nervous, I sounded squeaky.

You don't need to be nervous, I told myself. *So what if Rhys had a fling with her in college? That was over ten years ago. If he had liked her all that much back then, he would've stayed with her. Plus, she lied and hid a child from him, a child she claims she thought was his.*

She paused by the counter. "Haven, right?"

"Uh-huh."

"So how long have you been seeing Rhys?"

A sense of uneasiness unspooled inside me. I didn't trust Cathy and her questions, so I opted to be vague. "Oh, for a while."

She pursed her lips slightly, a knowing glint entering her gaze. "Hm, a while. For Rhys, a month would be a while. He had quite the reputation in college."

"College was a long time ago," I said pointedly.

Her eyes narrowed. I wasn't about to clue her in to my uncertainty and just how insecure I felt around her. She was, simply put, beautiful. Her silky smooth corn-flower-blond hair fell halfway down her back. Her blue eyes were wide, and her features were clean and tidy with a straight nose, elegant cheekbones, and mani-cured brows.

I felt short and frumpy beside her. She had the kind of build where clothes draped elegantly off her shoulders, and she never had to worry about her curves being too much.

I shifted on my feet, annoyed that I had to look up to meet her gaze.

"I suppose so, but you don't really seem his type."

"I don't see how you would even know." Then I went and said something shitty, something that immediately sent a flush of embarrassment through me. "Although you definitely had a type, seeing as you were involved with both Rhys and his brother."

Cathy's eyes went from calculating to icy. Her shoulders stiffened, and two bright red spots appeared on her cheeks. "Wow, I suppose the whole 'college was a long time ago' doesn't apply to me."

I threw a hand up in the air, letting it fall. "I don't know you, Cathy. We met once, and you just now pretended as if you weren't sure what my name was. I've known Rhys for as long as I can remember because we both grew up here and he's best friends with my brother. No matter what you think of him and me, or frankly what I might think of you, choosing to hide a child from his family was hurtful. Don't be surprised if most people who know them question your motives. Just be decent." I took a sharp breath. "I apologize for my comment."

With that, I turned and left the bathroom, lifting my chin as I walked past her. She looked startled. I honestly didn't want to try to be friends with her. I would be polite, but I didn't trust her motives until she proved otherwise.

When I got to the register, Hazel was handing some change over to a couple. They thanked her as they lifted their coffees off the counter and walked to the only empty table over in the corner. She glanced at me before turning to wipe down the espresso machine. "Are you okay? If we hadn't had any customers, I would've followed Cathy into the bathroom."

"I'm fine. I don't trust her," I said under my breath as I picked up a clean towel from the stack on the shelving underneath the counter.

"I don't trust her either."

A moment later, Cathy came out of the bathroom. For a second, I thought she was going to leave the café entirely, but she didn't. She smoothed her hands down her slacks and approached the counter. The only way to describe how she looked was chastened. She wore a tight smile when she stopped in front of the register.

"What can I get for you?" I asked courteously.

Although I still felt uncertain around her, and my old insecurities clamored loudly inside me, I was relieved I had been honest with her. That truth wasn't just for me. It was for Rhys, for all of his family.

"I'll have a chai tea," Cathy said.

"Coming right up," Hazel said brightly beside me.

I tapped on the register's computer screen. "That'll be three fifty."

Cathy paid, and I gave her the change. She stuffed the change in the tip jar as Hazel passed over her drink and left without another word.

"What the hell did you say to her?" Hazel murmured under her breath.

"The truth. She commented on the way Rhys was in college after asking how long we'd been together." I shook my head. "I told her that she needed to understand people might not trust her because she hid a child from the whole family. Of course, then I made a shitty comment and had to apologize." My cheeks burned.

Hazel's brows flew up. "What did you say?"

"When she said I wasn't Rhys's type, I pointed out that *she* obviously had a type since she was involved with Jake and Rhys in college."

Hazel's mouth dropped open. "Oh, my word," she breathed.

Chapter Twenty-Six

HAVEN

Rhys had texted me that he had a board meeting that evening, so he'd be working late. These meetings occurred monthly, and I knew he would usually be at work late.

For me, that meant an evening working on my other job. I needed to look at rates for the kind of work McKenna wanted. I sent a message to a friend of mine back in Boston. She also did invitations for weddings, baby showers, and so on, but her business had expanded.

After that, I typed up some pricing to review with McKenna. Meanwhile, something I'd been trying to ignore had to be dealt with. I was two weeks late for my period, which made no sense.

I reread the text message from my doctor. *The only suggestion I can make is for you to do a pregnancy test. Because that's what we would do here at the office. It's more expensive to come here and have us do it than it is for you to pick one up at the pharmacy.*

I stared at my purse where it sat innocuously on the coffee table. With a sigh, I slid my laptop off my lap, setting it on the coffee table, and trading it for my purse. I took two pregnancy test boxes out and stood there staring at one in my hand.

"Oh my God. I can't believe I'm doing this," I breathed. "It's a fluke. It has to be."

I walked into the kitchen as I opened the slender box. Removing the small handheld plastic test, I read the instructions quickly.

"If it turns blue, I'm pregnant," I said aloud.

Anxiety twisted in my belly, and I felt nervous and antsy.

I'd been waiting because I kept thinking I would get my period. I was on birth control. I had exactly zero plans to get pregnant. What would Rhys think? If I was pregnant, should I have the baby? Did I want to have a baby?

"Oh my God, I'm freaking out," I said to no one.

I talked to myself often when I was nervous. It was convenient Rhys had a board meeting tonight. If I were pregnant, I'd have several hours to get my shit together.

Of course, my doctor had also pointed out via text that the test may not show as positive just yet, and I may need to try again in another two weeks.

I managed the awkward task of holding the plastic stick underneath me while I peed. I placed the test on the counter by the sink as I washed my hands. It said to wait for five minutes, so I set a timer on my watch. After darting out of the bathroom, I crossed my arms and paced in a small circle in the living room.

As soon as the timer went off, I stopped pacing, unfolded my arms, and shook them as if I could discharge the nervous adrenaline racing through me. I walked into the bathroom, my gaze trained on the tiled floor. Almost as if I didn't look, whatever the results showed couldn't be true.

On the heels of a shaky deep breath, I lifted my gaze to the pregnancy test waiting on the counter. I felt the blood drain from my face. I sat down abruptly on the closed toilet, my hand gripping the edge of the counter. After several deep breaths, I uncurled my hand and reached for the pregnancy test, staring at the bright blue plus sign.

Oh my God. Oh my God. Oh my God.

I told myself it was ridiculous at the time, but I'd bought two tests, just to be double sure of the results.

My legs felt wobbly as I walked back into the living room and fetched the other test off the coffee table. Ripping the packaging open, I returned to the bathroom. Moments later, I walked back out into the living room, crossing my arms and pacing in a tight circle once again until the timer went off.

This time, I was calmer when I walked back into the bathroom and almost resigned when I saw the blue plus sign staring back at me. I sat down on the side of the tub. Resting my elbows on my knees, I dropped my face into my hands and let out a shaky sigh.

I ran my hands through my hair before lifting my head.

Chapter Twenty-Seven

HAVEN

I was so wound up inside and discombobulated by this startling development that I couldn't calm down. I must've paced around my small house for a good fifteen minutes. I circled from the corner of the kitchen counter to the front windows and back again.

I finally jumped in the shower, hoping the shock of some cold water followed by hot would snap my mind out of its spinning uncertainty and near panic. As I stood under the water, my mind volleyed thoughts back and forth.

How could this happen? I'm on birth control.

Things happen. It's not 100 percent.

Fuck, fuck, fuck. What am I going to tell Rhys?

Whenever I wondered how Rhys might react, the uncertainty wound tighter and tighter inside me. I wasn't even ready to talk about this. I needed to know what I wanted to do first.

I felt like Rhys and I were just getting back to a good place. In all honesty, I had some regret over how strongly I'd reacted to the potential news that Rhys had a child somewhere in the world and hadn't told me about it. Ever since that turned out not to be the case, twinges of guilt stung inside. Yet I felt like the break had been necessary for us.

Maybe he didn't understand, but we had tumbled into our fling rapidly. While I had plenty of doubts about relationships, and frankly about Rhys genuinely wanting to be serious with anyone, including me, I also felt there had been—I didn't know how to put words to it—almost a thin veil between us.

I didn't doubt the chemistry burning like a bonfire between us. But Rhys had plenty of emotional baggage. Because of my brother's friendship with him, I didn't have any illusions that his family was perfect. Even before Jake died in college, I knew things weren't great.

He and his siblings were good people and cared deeply for each other. Their mother was wonderful, but their grandfather had been horrible. On a few occasions, I'd seen how verbally harsh he could be. What happened to Jake was tragic. That had revealed the whole truth about just what a toxic and abusive man their grandfather had been.

Rhys was honest about that history. I sensed the wounds of it cut deeply—for him as well as for the whole family. He held a part of himself back, and I hadn't wanted to think about it. The start of our relationship had been like opening a bottle of champagne —fizzy and showy, it had felt *soooo* good. Because I knew him, there was a comfort, a trust there. I'd overlooked some of what I knew might be in the way for both of us.

After I showered, I changed into comfortable clothes. I turned on the television and settled in to watch a few episodes of *Schitt's Creek*, my favorite comfort distraction. I put the news of my unexpected pregnancy into a little closet in my brain. I wasn't ready to talk with Rhys about it, and I experienced a twinge of guilt about that. I just needed some time.

I was startled by the emotion tied up inside me. I was surprised to discover a part of me wanted this baby. The thought of having children hadn't even been on my radar yet. The idea of family and children and commitment were distant concepts. I'd thought maybe someday I'd have kids. That was as far as my thinking had gone.

The reality of those pregnancy tests tossed in the trash can felt like choppy waves slapping at me, reminding me what was *very* real.

Despite the jumbled thoughts bouncing around in my brain, I still felt that familiar sense of anticipation when Rhys texted that he was on his way home from his board meeting. When he got there, I was the one who sought to lose myself in our connection.

After he shrugged off his jacket and kicked off his shoes, I caught one of his hands in mine and peered up at him. His hair was mussed as if he had run his hand through it a few too many times. His gaze was alert yet a bit subdued.

"How are you?" I asked.

"Glad to be here. Long day."

He was standing by the couch and gave my hand a little tug, reeling me closer to him. He lifted a hand and brushed a few wayward curls away from my forehead.

I smiled at him, leaning up to press a kiss just under the edge of his jaw. His hand slid into my hair, sifting through my curls before his palm rested softly on the back of my neck. I could feel where each fingertip landed, the subtle warmth of his touch drifting through me, throwing sparks into an already hot fire.

This was precisely why it had been so easy for me to tumble into this unexpected relationship with Rhys. Our chemistry was like banked coals. Nothing more than a subtle touch or a look sent the flames leaping.

"Haven," he murmured.

I pressed another kiss underneath his jaw. I could feel his arousal cradled against my low belly. I *needed* this connection with him. I *needed* to lose myself in us and get singed by this fire.

Reaching between us, I molded my palm over the hard length of his arousal before swiftly unbuttoning his jeans. When I slid my palm into his boxers, curling around the hot, silky length of him, he rasped, "Haven, I need you."

I stepped back, just slightly, pushing his hips into the back of the couch. "I'm all yours, but first, this." I teased my thumb over the tip of his cock, sliding it over the drop of pre-cum rolling out.

He let out something between a moan and a growl when I shoved his jeans and boxers down just far enough for his cock to spring free. I swirled my tongue around the thick crown, savoring the way his fingers tightened in my hair. When I peered up at him as I angled my head to the side and dragged my tongue along the underside of his cock, the dark, intent look in his eyes sent heat pooling in my belly. I could feel my arousal slick between my thighs.

I teased the tip of his cock with my tongue before sucking him in, need cracking like a whip through my body at the earthy, salty flavor of him. I cupped his balls lightly as I licked and sucked before shifting my palm up to curl around his thick, swollen shaft.

"Haven," he bit out, his tone almost a warning.

I leaned back, releasing him with a slippery pop as I looked up at him, just before swirling my tongue around his crown again. "Just a sec," I whispered.

When I sucked him in deeply again, his fingers laced more tightly in my hair, creating a subtle sting on my scalp as he came in spurts into my mouth. I waited until his fingers loosened before I drew back, biting my lip as I straightened.

"Your turn," he said after a moment.

His hands fell free from my hair, one palm falling to my hip and slipping under the hem of my soft, fleece sweatshirt. Rhys knew how to make me crazy and proceeded to do so with deliberation.

Sometime later, after he left me boneless and sated against him, I rested on his lap on the couch. My clothes were strewn on the floor, while his shirt was merely unbuttoned, and he never got his jeans all the way off.

His palm moved in a lazy pass down my spine as his lips pressed hot, open-mouthed kisses along my collarbone. I didn't even let myself think about what I wasn't telling him.

Chapter Twenty-Eight

RHYS

"Well, what do you think?" my sister asked.

"I think it's a great idea. I've seen Haven's work. She's excellent."

"Are you sure you're not saying that just because you're whipped?" my brother Adam asked as he stopped beside me where I sat on one of the stools lining the island in our mother's kitchen.

I slid my eyes to his and shook my head. "No. If her work wasn't good, I wouldn't recommend McKenna hire her."

"As if you have a say in who I hire to handle stuff," McKenna retorted, lifting her arm and dragging the back of her sleeve across her forehead to get a loose lock of hair out of her eyes as she finished chopping the onions.

I grinned over at her. "True, I don't stick my nose in that kind of thing. But if Haven's work wasn't good, I would probably point it out. Because it could get complicated if we hired someone connected to the family and the reasons weren't valid."

Adam chuckled, rolling his eyes.

"Things are going to work out for you and Haven, right?" McKenna pressed as she lifted the cutting board and carefully used the back of the knife to slide the onions into the pan on the oven, the oil snapping and crackling underneath.

I narrowed my eyes at Adam before glancing back at McKenna. "Yes," I said firmly. "Things will work out with Haven."

Blake entered the kitchen, catching the tail end of my comment. "Not if Cathy has anything to say about it," he said with a smirk as he crossed over to the refrigerator, opening it and pulling out a beer for himself.

"Mind grabbing me one of those?" Kenan called over as he came walking in behind Blake.

Blake caught the edge of the refrigerator door before it closed and snagged another bottle of beer, calling over his shoulder, "Should I just get the whole six-pack out?"

"That'd be the smart move," Adam replied with a quick chuckle.

Blake set the beer on the counter beside my elbow. I caught his eyes as I reached for a bottle. "I don't really give a shit what Cathy thinks."

McKenna looked curiously between us. Adam shook his head slightly as he twisted off the bottle cap and tossed it in the trash under the counter. "I don't think any of us do. I don't trust her. And, honestly, I'm a little annoyed that we offered her any money."

"The money's not for her," I replied. "It's for Matthew. I had them set it up pretty tightly controlled. She can only use it for expenses for him. The trust is set up so he can't access it until he's twenty-five. Even then, it's managed."

"I know, but I don't like it. Sure, we can say it's

only for his expenses, but she'll use it for whatever she wants. It's pretty generous," Adam countered.

"I don't care about the money," McKenna interjected. "What are you talking about with Cathy?"

I took a swallow of beer before replying, "Blake told me he thought Cathy was after me. I don't know if she's really after me, but she's flirting. I'm ignoring it."

"Why would she do that? You're in a relationship with Haven." McKenna rested a hand on her hip as she stirred the onions in the pan with her other hand.

Blake waggled his eyebrows. "Because she's not stupid. If she can get her claws into Rhys, her financial options are much more lucrative."

McKenna let out a huff. "If she's working that angle, she should try one of the other brothers."

Kenan nearly spit his beer out. He snagged a napkin and dragged it across his mouth before offering, "Clearly, she doesn't realize we're a close family. We're all ruled out at this point. I have no doubt neither Jake nor Rhys would've been interested back in college if you'd known she was screwing around with both of you."

"Definitely not," I replied dryly.

The mention of Jake's name sent a chill through the teasing conversation. We all missed him. I'd give anything to have him here, and I knew any of my siblings would as well.

"That's weird," McKenna said softly as she adjusted the temperature under the pan and turned to reach for a bowl of sliced chicken. She added the chicken and began stirring again.

"What's weird?" Griffin asked as he came walking in.

"Our nephew. I don't mean he's weird," McKenna

clarified. "Just that he's Jake's son, and Jake's not here. I miss him."

Griffin stopped beside her, sliding his arm around her shoulders and squeezing gently. "We all do."

Sometimes when I thought about Jake being gone, I had to remind myself that, except for Blake and me, our other siblings had been so much younger when he died. McKenna was thirteen when he passed. Wyatt and Griffin had been fourteen.

Our mother had wanted a big family because she'd been an only child. She always said it was lucky that twins ran in her family, and she had two sets of them. After my father passed away, it was just her trying to juggle all of us.

Jake and I had been close. I was relieved Blake and I had also been tight because he understood how it had been before, as did Adam and Kenan. It wasn't that Wyatt, Griffin, and McKenna didn't. It was just that their relationship with Jake was different because there had been more years between them.

"We all do," I said quietly.

"Seriously," Blake chimed in.

I looked around the room and realized only one of us was missing—Wyatt. He was the only one of us who kept his distance. He didn't want to be part of the business and hadn't lived in Fireweed Harbor since he left for college. Like Wyatt, Griffin was usually up in Fairbanks with Deacon hotshot firefighting, but he'd come home for the weekend to meet Matthew.

Blake stopped at the counter, sliding his hips onto the stool beside me and lifting his beer bottle aloft. "To Jake."

A moment later, we clicked our bottles together with McKenna tapping her spatula against them. Shortly after that, our mom came walking in. The conversation had moved on, which was probably for the best. Ever since Cathy had shown up with Matthew, our mother's grief surrounding Jake had been more present. But then, she had always worn her heart on her sleeve. She'd had more than her share of loss—between our dad passing, and the effect that had on our family with our grandfather's damage, and then Jake dying and eventually learning the full truth of what our grandfather had done. Now, years later, there was no way for him to truly answer for that. I was just grateful he'd gotten nailed for embezzlement even though it had been from our own company.

My mother smiled around the room. "We need to get Wyatt home," she said softly.

Kenan rested his elbows on the counter as he grinned at our mother. "You know he'll be here when he can."

What went unspoken was that Wyatt obviously could be here if he chose. Yet he wasn't.

My mother stopped beside me as the conversation carried on around us a few minutes later. Her eyes studied me. "Cathy told me she'll be staying for another two weeks."

"Okay." I waited.

"I know we can't expect her to move here, but a part of me wishes she would."

"You can travel for visits when you'd like."

Seeing as I'd been trying to keep my distance from Cathy, we hadn't chatted much. I didn't necessarily expect her to come to Fireweed Harbor often. Aside from visits for Matthew, there was nothing to bring her here.

I studied my mother briefly, sliding my arm around her shoulders. "I know you wish Jake was here."

Her eyes glistened with tears. She looked down,

and I could feel her shoulders rise with a deep breath. She looked back up at me. "I always miss Jake. Matthew brings a lot of old feelings to the surface."

"For all of us."

———

We had dinner, and it was the usual slightly messy affair with conversation bouncing around the table. As I was leaving later, my phone vibrated with a text. I slipped it out of my pocket to glance down at the screen.

Yet again, Cathy had texted me.

Cathy: *Just wondering if we could get together, maybe for dinner?*

I ignored it, resolving to answer in the morning.

Chapter Twenty-Nine

HAVEN

A few days later

Rhys was in the shower. He had come over last night after dinner with his family, something they did every few weeks. I loved that about their family. On occasion, I joined them, but not always. Rhys had invited me last night, but I needed to finalize some custom wedding invitations.

His phone vibrated on the counter just beside the coffee maker where he had left it. I wasn't even trying to snoop, but I glanced down reflexively and saw Cathy's name on the screen.

Cathy: *You haven't replied. Could you let me know when I can see you?*

All of my insecurities rushed forward, as if they'd been waiting for this very moment to remind me that Rhys and Cathy had been involved once upon a time. To remind me that she was beautiful and stunning. To remind me that maybe, just maybe, Rhys wasn't cut out for something serious. At least not with me.

We didn't hide our phones from each other, and I knew his password. Before I could think better of it, I had typed it in and opened up the series of texts with Cathy.

It's nothing, I told myself. *He hasn't agreed to have dinner with her.*

But what if they did have dinner?

And I just didn't know about it?

I felt a little sick and mortified that I had stooped to snooping in his phone. I quickly closed the text screen and put his phone back on the counter.

A few minutes later, Rhys had come out and was getting ready to leave. "Can we walk in together?" he asked.

"Sure!" My voice was a little too cheery and bright sounding.

I savored our walks in together. But this morning, I was anxious with a ball of dread, nervousness, and insecurity tightening in my gut.

At the café, Rhys gave me a lingering kiss. I watched him depart and pressed two fingers to my lips as if I could hold his kiss there.

Chapter Thirty

RHYS

Late morning the same day

When I got in my SUV, I glanced in the rearview mirror. I'd forgotten that I had Haven's and my recycling to drop off at the recycling center. I had time, just enough, to swing by there before I went to the winery.

A short drive later, I emptied the bins. I was just turning away when my eyes snagged on a pink box. Even now, I couldn't say why I turned back and reached for it.

It was a box for a pregnancy test. There were two of them.

What the hell?

Chapter Thirty-One

HAVEN

My day was blessedly busy. As the weather got warmer and the days got longer, it wasn't just the cruise ships that kept Fireweed Harbor busy. Seasonal workers poured into town for fishing and touristy jobs. The population of our little town quadrupled in the summers. When I thought about growing up here, I remembered loving the summers and winters. Summer days felt like they lasted forever with energy and laughter buzzing in the air, while winter felt cozy with snow blanketing the world. You felt part of a special place in the winter because not everybody stayed. The town felt small and knitted together by the shared joy of living on the edge of the wilderness.

By the time I had a chance to catch my breath, I hadn't checked my phone in hours. Phyllis waved me away, insisting I should take a long break. Between my worries about Cathy and the giant secret I was keeping from Rhys, the busyness had been a relief because I didn't have time to think.

I headed into the back, walking past Hazel, who was training a new high school girl for the afternoon shifts. I slipped into the small break room in the back. It was tucked just behind the ovens and was the only place where the sound from the front was muted. After closing the door, I untied my apron from my waist, hanging it on the back of the chair before stepping into the bathroom. The staff bathroom was tiny, which was why most of us used the front bathroom when we were out there. This one had just enough room for a sink and the toilet and nothing more. Moments later, I sat down at the table and snagged one of the day-old savory pastries.

Only then did I look at my phone, sliding it out of my pocket to see three texts from Rhys.

Rhys: *Remember how I told you I'd drop off your recycling?*

Fifteen minutes later.

Rhys: *I loaded it up last night. I forgot to take my car this morning because we walked in together, so I walked back to get it. Why do you have two pregnancy test boxes in your recycling?*

Twenty minutes later.

Rhys: *What the hell aren't you telling me?*

The blood drained from my face, and I felt sick. Between my twinges of guilt and embarrassment and uncertainty and insecurity battling with my secret inside, I knew I'd fucked up. I should've told him right away.

"Are you okay?" Hazel's voice came through the doorway.

I glanced over, having no idea how long she'd been standing there.

"Not really," I blurted out. I set my phone down and took a shaky breath.

"What's going on?" She stepped into the room,

closing the door before sitting across from me at the small round table.

"I'm pregnant, and I didn't tell Rhys because I wanted time to figure out how I felt. He took my recycling in this morning and saw the boxes for the pregnancy tests." I was on a roll, and everything tumbled out. "I saw this weird, vague text from Cathy on his phone, and I snooped. I'm freaking out and worried that maybe he likes her, or something's going on and I don't know about it."

It was near impossible to hide things from Hazel. She was truly like a dog with a bone when she sensed something was off with anyone she cared about. Also, I really needed some advice.

Hazel was quiet for a beat before saying, "Breathe."

I took another shaky breath. She stood, holding her finger up. "I'll be right back. You need something sweet."

She dashed out of the room. A moment later, she returned with a mug, handing it over. "It's the extra sweet chai tea. A little bit of sugar helps with this kind of shock," she assured me. "Take a sip."

I did, instantly realizing she was right. The hit of sugar helped me a little.

She sat down again, her gaze calm. "Before we get into whether you want to have this baby, you don't owe Rhys an instant explanation if you're pregnant. You get to decide when you tell him. I know you're trying to work things out, and I respect all that, but it's not like you have to tell him immediately. Were you trying to get pregnant?"

I shook my head swiftly. "I'm on birth control."

She nodded matter-of-factly. "Okay, so it's a surprise. Do you want to have a baby?"

"I haven't even been thinking about it, so I'm not

sure. I wanted to have a conversation with him about it, but I just hadn't gotten around to it yet. I wasn't ready."

"So that's exactly what you're going to say to him. Now, Cathy. Nothing is going on with Rhys and Cathy. Except for her trying to make something go on."

I opened my mouth to protest.

She held her palm up. "Shut up and listen."

I let out a dry laugh, lifting my mug of chai tea and taking a healthy swallow.

"You're not here all the time. Cathy came in one time when Rhys was here for his afternoon coffee. I think she's trying to make a play for him. I don't even know if she actually likes him. I think she's after his money, and that's fine. She'll get some of it because she has Jake's son. But Rhys is about as interested in her as he is in watching paint dry. He also doesn't trust her. For a good reason. No matter what she did or didn't know about their family back in college, she knew they were brothers. All you had to do was see them to know that. She hid this baby from them. Maybe she had her reasons, and we don't understand them. That's fine. But she should come clean now. It sounds like what you saw was vague, so don't put the word spin on it. Talk to Rhys about this and talk to him about seeing the text."

"I'm mortified that I looked in his phone. I'm embarrassed even telling you," I admitted.

Hazel waved a hand dismissively. "I don't judge you for it. I even understand you feeling a little insecure. Cathy is beautiful, but so are you. And you're way more interesting than her. She's kind of boring as far as looks go."

I snorted.

"Reply to his text, or go see him right now."

"Now?" I yelped.

"Now. If you don't, you'll just be freaking out until you talk to him."

She had a point. I found myself walking down the street to the office building for Fireweed Industries only minutes later. It was only a five-minute walk from the coffee shop. The receptionist waved me upstairs when I got there.

Rhys's office door was open, and I approached it, coming to an abrupt stop when I heard Cathy's voice. There she stood, immediately in front of Rhys. She had her palm on his chest, looking up at him.

Cathy glanced over. The moment she saw me, she smirked. Rhys whipped toward the doorway, his eyes narrowing as he caught the look on Cathy's face. "Haven—" He began.

I shook my head quickly. My emotions were a jumble inside—anger, jealousy, hurt, and shame that I'd even put myself in this position. "I have to go."

I never even walked through the door, racing down the stairs from where I'd come. I just wanted to get out of there. I didn't have it in me to have a conversation in front of Cathy. Under the best of circumstances, it would be awkward.

The sound of my footsteps on the stairs was loud. I felt like I couldn't move fast enough when I heard Rhys call my name again as he followed me. I stopped at the base of the stairs, turning to see him approaching.

"Haven. Please, let's talk."

I shook my head. "You obviously have other priorities."

Chapter Thirty-Two

RHYS

"Rhys," Cathy said from behind me.

I wanted to catch up with Haven to explain. Not that there was anything to explain. But I knew how it might look. I also knew Cathy was a master of creating an impression and that little moment had given her something to work with.

Haven was gone, and chasing after her wouldn't fix this, so I turned back. Without a word, I strode quickly past Cathy and into my office. I resisted the urge to slam the door shut in her face, solely because I had something to say to her.

She was right behind me, but when she reached to close the door, I caught it with my hand. "No."

She took a step, stopping immediately in front of me. I let my gaze coast over her face, dispassionately noting how pretty she was. Yet I felt nothing. I was no longer a young college guy looking for nothing more than a good time with no strings attached.

Although Matthew wasn't my son, he was my nephew. My brief entanglement with Cathy in college had resulted in unforeseen consequences. My life would be forever connected to her. I wasn't worried about ever being attracted to her again, but I was stuck dealing with our connection.

She lifted her hand, placing it on my upper arm, her touch light and gentle. "Rhys, I don't know what's going on with you and Haven—"

I cut her off. "I love Haven."

Cathy arched a manicured brow. "Clearly, things aren't that great. All she had to do was see me, and it's obvious she feels threatened. It's not that I don't understand. We *did* have a relationship before."

I shook her hand away and took a step back, making it clear that I wanted the physical distance between us. "Cathy, we did *not* have a relationship. We spent a few nights together. Nothing more. You were also involved with my brother at the same time. I don't know what you knew about our family then, but clearly, you decided to come calling when you wanted some money."

Two bright red spots crested high on her cheeks. Her gaze shifted from calculated flirtation to cool and annoyed. "I can't believe you're judging me. You were known for never being serious with anyone in college. How was I to know you and Jake were brothers?"

I rolled my eyes. "Because we looked so much alike, people sometimes confused us for twins. The only thing I judge you for is withholding a major piece of information. You'll never admit it, but I doubt you knew about our family situation back then because we were careful not to talk about it. When you found out, you decided to cash in. For what it's worth, I really don't care about the money. I understand that not caring about money is a privilege, but it burns to know you couldn't bother to make sure your son knew his father's family before now. Don't you dare try to interfere with Haven and me. If you don't stay civil and let Matthew maintain a relationship with my mother, we will redo the legal paperwork. Jake is dead. You're not entitled to anything except survivor's benefits."

Cathy lifted her chin, her jaw tightening as she stared at me. "Think whatever you want. I wish you would give *us* an opportunity. Maybe it was brief, but we were good together."

I shook my head. "Never going to happen."

Blessedly, the sound of footsteps approaching in the hallway reached us. Cathy laced her hands together. The only giveaway that she was still angry was her knuckles whitening slightly.

Blake appeared in the doorway, his gaze bouncing from me to Cathy and back again.

"There you are," I said smoothly, knowing I could rely on my brother to follow my lead.

"Hey, hey," he said. "Sorry, I'm a few minutes behind."

"Come on in." I gestured him through the doorway, and he slipped passed Cathy. He dipped his chin in acknowledgment as he turned to face her when he stopped beside me.

"Good to see you. I heard from my mother you'll be flying out soon. We appreciate the opportunity to get to know Matthew," Blake said smoothly.

Cathy's nostrils flared when she took a slow breath. "Yes," she said, her voice level.

"Thank you all for being so welcoming. My flight leaves next week." Her eyes shifted to me. "I appreciate your time. I'll be going now."

"Have a good afternoon." That was all I could bring myself to say.

As soon as I heard her footsteps going down the stairs, I closed my office door, locking it for good measure. Blake's brows hitched up. "That seems like it was a pleasant conversation," he said dryly.

I walked across my office, plunking down in front of a small round table in the corner by the windows. I let out a ragged sigh. "I already admitted it, but I know you enjoy being right. You were right about Cathy." I leaned back in my chair.

"You look like you could use a drink," he observed as he sat down across from me.

My chuckle was dry. "I could." I glanced at my watch. "It's too early, though."

"What the hell just happened?"

"She sort of hit on me. Cathy is subtle, skilled enough that she could deny it. Unfortunately, Haven showed up. Cathy even smirked at her. After Haven took off, Cathy said she could understand why Haven might feel insecure about her."

"Fuuuu-ck," Blake said slowly.

I ran a hand through my hair, letting it drop with a thwack against the arm of the chair. "I'll talk to Haven later."

"You don't think Cathy would keep Matthew from Mom?"

"I made it clear that if she did, she would lose our financial support. It would be on her to go through the process of trying to get survivor's benefits."

"We're all glad to know Matthew, but it would really hurt Mom if she couldn't see him."

"I know," I said simply. "I don't think Cathy would do that. Anyway, what brings you by?"

Blake waggled his eyebrows. "Was wondering if maybe you could sit in on a few interviews with me?"

"For the new chef?"

"Yeah. David wants some of us there. I was

thinking you would be the harsh one. McKenna will be even more of a softy than me."

I let out a sharp laugh. "Sounds like a plan. Is he scheduling them now?" As the chef at the restaurant at the winery, David had managed that entirely for over twenty years.

"He said he was going to wait until next week, but he had a call from someone who's in town visiting and they have time to meet this afternoon. If you could come over for that"—he glanced at his watch— "around three?"

"You got it. You already confirmed with McKenna?"

My brother nodded. "Sure did. Need me to help run interference with Haven?"

"I have to deal with it myself."

Blake stood from his chair. "Understood. I have faith in you."

I rolled my eyes as I stood and walked him to the door. "I'll see you at three."

Chapter Thirty-Three

RHYS

I finally gave in. I'd sent Haven a few texts, but she hadn't replied. I couldn't wait all day to talk to her. I pocketed my keys and walked the block to Spill the Beans Café. When I walked in, it was busy.

We hadn't even talked about how she'd bolted after Cathy showed up at my office this morning. That felt like nothing now. The sight of two pregnancy test boxes in her recycling had banished that worry.

Hazel happened to be working the counter and glanced up with a smile. "Hi, Rhys. Here for your afternoon coffee?"

"Actually, I need to talk to Haven."

Haven approached the counter with a tray stacked with dishes. Hazel glanced from her to me, saying, "Well, she needs to go in the back and —"

"I'll talk to her in the back," I said through slightly gritted teeth, struggling to contain the jumble of emotions bouncing inside me.

Haven glanced over. Her eyes were wide. "I'm working, Rhys."

"I know. Did you get my texts?"

Her fingers tightened on the edge of the tray she was carrying. Hazel glanced back and forth between us, her gaze worried. "Are you okay?" she asked Haven.

Haven's cheeks were flushed as she nodded. She brushed past me to round the counter and go through the door into the back. I moved to follow her, but Hazel reached out, catching me by the elbow. Her grip was strong.

"Haven doesn't owe you an explanation," Hazel said firmly. I opened my mouth to argue the point, but the look in her eyes gave me pause. "She has every right to talk to you when she's ready. I'm just pointing that out before you go and get angry over something that you don't have a right to demand."

I forced myself to take a slow breath, letting it out in a controlled sigh. Hazel released my elbow. "I understand your point, but I love her."

Hazel studied me, and it felt as if she was kicking straight through my bullshit when she spoke. "I believe you love Haven, but I'm not so sure you're ready for what that means. Go on back." She gestured me toward the swinging door.

I pushed through, stopping when I got in the back and glancing around the space. One of the high school girls who worked here—I thought her name was Maggie—glanced over where she stood by the dishwasher, unloading clean dishes and stacking them neatly on shelves. She gestured toward the door at the back of the room. "Haven's in there."

I walked quickly across the room, stopping in front of the door. It was opened just slightly. My heart was beating hard, a drumroll of uncertainty and anxious anticipation echoing through me. I knocked lightly on the door. "Haven?"

The door swung open swiftly. "You didn't have to knock," she said sharply.

I followed her into the room, glancing around and taking in the space. I could see through another small doorway into what I presumed was the staff bathroom. A small round table sat in the center of the room with chairs around it. A counter containing a sink and a small dish rack was located opposite the bathroom.

Haven sat down at the table, gesturing across from her. "Sit," she ordered. She crossed her arms tightly.

I sat down, wondering where to begin, but she beat me to it. "I was going to talk to you. I'm pregnant. Obviously, I didn't expect this. I called my doctor this morning, and she said it can happen. She said sometimes the heat can decrease the effectiveness of birth control. I've only known since last week. My cycle is regular, so she guesses I'm only six weeks along." Haven's words came out rapidly.

I took it all in and sucked in a quick breath of air, bracing myself against the onslaught of this news. "Why didn't you talk to me?"

"Because I'm not sure yet what I want to do. I was panicking. I honestly didn't even think about getting pregnant. Why didn't you talk to me about Cathy? She's obviously interested in you."

We stared at each other, the silence between us crowded with emotions and frustration.

"Nothing is happening with Cathy." I was offended Haven thought that situation was even remotely in the ballpark of her hiding the fact that she was pregnant. "Clearly, you don't trust me. Let me know when you want to talk and be more honest."

Barely keeping myself in check, I stood and moved toward the door. I wasn't precisely sure what I felt.

Everything felt tangled up inside—anger she hadn't talked to me to begin with, hurt she was hiding it from me, hurt that she didn't trust me enough to talk, or trust me enough to let me know what was going on.

Haven stood, her arms unfolding. "Rhys—"

"I have to go."

I left, bottling that knotty mess of emotions and confusion up inside. Maybe Haven had been right before. We'd let our chemistry get the best of us.

When I walked outside, I almost collided with Cathy who was walking into the café.

"Oh!" She stepped back.

All I could do was brush past her. Her presence was a reminder of everything I hadn't gotten right yet.

As I walked toward Fireweed Winery, the one feeling I couldn't kick completely to the curb was this sneaky sense that maybe I was holding something back. Perhaps I was keeping a part of myself removed from Haven and feeding into her distrust.

No matter what it felt like, I couldn't do this. It was a mess, and I didn't know how to fix it.

Chapter Thirty-Four

RHYS

Aside from the fact I couldn't think straight, another problem with this interview was my appetite was nearly nonexistent.

Blake glanced over, one of his brows hitching up. "Well?"

"It's really good," I said. Maybe I didn't have an appetite, but I could tell the food was good. David had requested that the applicants create two dishes for the interview.

She'd created a twist on fried halibut bites, and she'd also made a wild Alaskan raspberry tart.

The interviewee, Fiona Blake, walked back into the room with David. Shockingly, he seemed to like her. We loved David, and he'd worked for the family for years, but he could be standoffish and was definitely *not* easy to impress.

He looked over at Blake, announcing, "We're hiring her."

Fiona had dark hair pulled back into a tight bun and was tidy and petite. She glanced from David to me to Blake. "Is this a group decision?" she asked carefully.

When Blake glanced her way, it was impossible to miss the way his eyes lingered on her mouth. He set down his plate. He seemed uncharacteristically guarded.

"If I don't want you, we won't hire you," David said firmly when she cast him an uncertain look.

I couldn't help but chuckle, relieved for something to snap through the cloud hanging over me since my discovery at the recycling center hours earlier.

I glanced at Fiona, shrugging lightly. "We're here for the interviews, but David runs the restaurant, so you answer to him."

David patted her lightly on the shoulder. "I have to get to work. You can let them handle the technicalities and pretend they're in charge."

Glancing at Blake, I asked, "What do we need to do? And where's McKenna?"

As if conjured by my question, McKenna appeared in the doorway. "Sorry I'm late!"

She hurried in, within minutes claiming that Fiona's samples were the best thing she'd ever tasted. After Fiona left, McKenna glanced at Blake. "Why don't you like her?"

"I like her just fine," he protested. "Even if I didn't, it doesn't matter. David runs the restaurant. The decision's already made." He glanced at me. "And what the hell is wrong with you? I thought you weren't in the best mood earlier, but now you're even worse."

"Haven is pregnant and didn't tell me about it."

Chapter Thirty-Five

HAVEN

"Okay, so what do you want to do?" Tessa asked. We were meeting for an emergency dinner at her house.

"Have you already decided? You're not having wine," Rosie said as she pointed at my glass of water before taking a healthy swallow of wine.

"I know." I leaned my elbows on the table, letting my head fall into my hands. My breath filtered through my fingers when I sighed. Straightening, I let my hands fall to the table with a thwack. "I think I want to keep the baby, and I can't even believe I'm saying that."

Tessa took a gulp of her wine before announcing, "I need to drink. This is stressful. Look, after what Rhys just went through with a possible son he didn't know was his, and now this? It's a little much."

Rosie shrugged. "Sure, but that's life. Also, what did your doctor say that might've affected your birth control?"

"When I asked her about it on the phone, she said sometimes the temperature in storage can decrease the effectiveness for birth control pills. Not that I'll ever know for sure, but I left my pills in the car one day when I picked them up on the way to work. It wasn't that hot outside, but my car was parked in the sun, so it was hot in the car, and they were in there all day. I just didn't even think about it." I took a gulp of my water.

"Most people wouldn't," Tessa pointed out. "Also, Hazel's right. You don't have to tell him anything. Women all over the world wait weeks before they decide to share this bit of news. I get why Rhys would be upset, but he has to deal."

"I just wasn't ready to talk about it, not until I knew what I wanted to do."

"That's fair," Rosie chimed in. "So what now?"

"Well, this threw me off. After he texted me, I went to Rhys's office and found Cathy with her hand on his chest. I'm pretty sure she was making a move. Between that and those texts..."

Tessa groaned. "I told you it was a bad idea to look through his phone. Everything's out of context. Hell, even people I've known a long time where there's nothing to even worry about, you can't capture the tone. That's why trying to interpret text messages is a terrible idea."

"I know. It's just the text showed up on the screen, and then I was freaking out—"

Tessa circled her hand in the air, adding, "Blah, blah, blah. You and the universe looking at each other's phones. Just talk to him. Plus, I've seen Cathy." She tsk-tsked. "She's *that* kind of woman."

"What do you mean?"

"I bet she doesn't have many, if any, female friends. She's always hedging her bets. We already know she was involved with both Rhys and Jake in college. I don't care what anyone says. Those guys were practically twins, so there's no way she didn't know they were brothers. I'm not into slut shaming, so that's not what this is about, but it's a little, uh, bold to be involved with two brothers, and they didn't know about it."

"My guess is once she realized she might have a nice meal ticket here, she went for it," Rosie piped up. "Maybe she was being honest when she said she genuinely thought Rhys was the more likely father. But he's not. The family doesn't owe her anything, but they're giving her something anyway. It's all tied up for her son, not her, so she makes a move on Rhys. She could go for one of the other brothers, but—"

Tessa burst out laughing. "That would just feel like too much."

I let out another sigh, feeling weary of my sighs. I glanced at the wine bottle in the center of the table. "I wish I could have wine."

"We cannot drink in solidarity," Rosie pointed out.

I waved a hand dismissively in the air. "I can handle myself. So what do I do?"

"You give it a few days and try to talk to Rhys," Tessa said.

"A few days?"

"You avoided him for a month after you accidentally got served that legal paperwork," Rosie reminded.

"This is kind of heavy news for him to find out by accident. I'm all about a time-out," Tessa said.

I let out a laugh as I looked over at her. "Seriously?"

"Yeah, it's a way for everybody to cool off. I give myself a time-out sometimes when I'm ready to scream at school." Tessa taught first graders, and while

she loved it, she also enjoyed regaling us with hyster-
ical stories about mishaps in her class.

"Rhys needs a few days to adjust to the news. Give
him some time to cool down, and I'm sure someone in
his family will help him see things rationally," Rosie
interjected. "Meanwhile, that'll give you time to think
about things. And also, fuck Cathy. I'm going to do
some reconnaissance."

"Reconnaissance?" Tessa prompted.

"Yes. I'm not worried about Rhys wanting Cathy,
but I'd like to find out just what the hell she's up to
and when she's leaving town. I'm also going to tell her
to stay the fuck away from him," Rosie said firmly.

"You can't exactly do that," I said. "Matthew is his
nephew, and Rhys's mom really wants to have a relationship with her grandson."

"Cathy's not stupid. She won't ruin the money situation when they don't have to give her anything. She
knows she needs to maintain at least some kind of
decent relationship."

"How long is a few days?"

"Three," my friends said in unison.

Chapter Thirty-Six

RHYS

Two whole days passed. I'd only received one text from Haven.

Haven: *We have a lot to talk about. But I'm trying to respect that this news is probably big for you. I know it's huge for me. Let's take a few days. If you need more than that, let me know. I love you.*

I must've read that text over a hundred times. I still hadn't replied.

"Rhys!" Blake called from the brewing area.

I'd been standing in the hallway at the back staff entrance. Turning, I waved as I resumed walking. "How's it going?" I asked when I stopped in the doorway.

Blake finished drying his hands on a towel and tossed it into a basket by the doorway when he stopped in front of me. "Busy. Thought you were stuck out there. It was like a glitch in a video game."

I chuckled. "This is real life, and I wasn't stuck."

He studied me for a moment, his gaze sobering. "You done being mad at Haven yet?"

"It's more complicated than being mad."

"Is it, though?" he asked lightly. I stepped into the room. "Follow me." He waved for me to walk with him. "Your workday is done. You might as well have a beer with me."

I followed him over to a small table in the corner of the room. "I need some advice." He brought out several glasses and handed me a notepad.

"Oh, am I giving you opinions?"

"Not on the beer, some samples from Fiona. David keeps asking us for feedback as they revise the menu. Be right back."

While Blake went to get the samples, I stood from the table and walked over to fetch a beer out of the private refrigerator we kept back here. I also snagged a few bottles of water.

"Mind getting one for me?"

I glanced over to see my brother Kenan coming in through the doorway.

"Any requests?"

He shook his head. "Whatever your hand lands on."

I grabbed another bottle of beer and met him back at the table, where we sat down together.

"What are the plates for?" he asked, taking the beer bottle from me as I slid it across the table to him.

"Apparently, we're taste testing for the new chef." I twisted the cap off my beer, eyeing the label. "What did I get you?" I asked as I lifted my gaze to my brother.

He read the label. "A honey stout. What do you have?"

"Chocolate porter." I took a swallow, savoring the hint of chocolate and the rich flavor.

"That's one of my faves. I'm partial to the honey

stout, though," Kenan said before taking a swallow of his beer. "Have you met the new chef?"

"Yeah, McKenna and I were here for the interview. David wanted to hire her, so the decision was easy."

"He's difficult to please."

"No shit." I rolled my eyes.

"What did you think of her?" he asked.

"The food samples were good. If David likes her, I'm sure the food will be good. I have one concern."

"What's that?"

"Blake was tense around her. Not as friendly as he usually is." I drummed my fingertips on the table and took a swallow of beer. "She's kind of prim. Uptight isn't quite the word, but we'll see how she fits in here. He pretended he wasn't worried about anything."

Kenan shrugged. "Not our problem. As long as her food is good, everything else will fall into place. David's in charge of the restaurant anyway. Blake has worked with him for years, but he doesn't try to interfere."

Just then, Blake reappeared, carrying a tray from the kitchen with a stand in the other hand.

"Damn, my timing was excellent," Kenan teased as Blake stopped by the table.

I opened the stand for him, and he lowered the full tray onto it. "Dude, there's enough food there for five people," I pointed out. "Not that I'm complaining. Everything looks really good."

Ever since the news about Haven's pregnancy, I'd been swinging between no appetite and starving. At the moment, I was famished.

Blake waggled his brows as he sat down with us. He glanced at our bottles of beer. "You didn't get me one?"

"On it." I stood and quickly jogged over to the

refrigerator, blindly grabbing another bottle of beer and returning to the table.

"Mmm, the oatmeal stout," Blake mused. "One of our longtime staples. I enjoy trying the new stuff, but what sells is what sells. This stout sells well year after year after year."

"Oldie but goodie," Kenan chimed in. "How long do I have to wait to eat?"

Blake snorted a laugh, taking a quick swallow from his beer before standing. "Consider this our buffet. Just take your pick."

Moments later, we'd transferred all the plates to the center of the table. "This is what I call an array," Kenan said as he piled his plate with food. "How is David handling training with her?"

Blake paused as he finished chewing a bite. "Surprisingly well. And it's kind of weird. You know how he likes people to suck up to him?"

"Oh yeah. You had to do a lot of that to get on his good side when you took over here," I pointed out.

Blake snorted. "True. Fiona doesn't suck up to him. She's all business."

"You don't seem too sure about her," Kenan offered. He bit into something and let out a moan. After he finished chewing, he added, "Her food is fucking amazing."

"Exactly." Blake swung his arm in an arc across the table. "I'm just not sure how she's going to fit in. David has been running the show since this place started. It's kind of freewheeling. She's, uh, uptight, I guess."

"David likes her, so I'm sure it'll be fine. How long until he steps back from the kitchen?"

"It's his call. He's not leaving, just shifting solely to admin. I could push it and tell him when."

"He'll make your life hell if you do," I cut in.

"Trust the process. I trust David's judgment," Kenan said.

At that moment, Fiona appeared in the doorway. Once again, her hair was pulled tightly back, this time in a high ponytail that hung halfway down her back. She glanced over at us.

"David said to come back here to ask you where to get any of the beer and wine we can use for cooking?" Her voice lilted with a question at the end.

Blake stood, quickly wiping his hands on a napkin. "Sure thing, right over here."

Fiona entered the room. I couldn't help but notice the way Blake's eyes lingered on her when she glanced around.

"This refrigerator." He tapped one of the refrigerators against the wall. He then pointed at the one beside it. "If you ever want something to take home, go for it." He gestured to a wine cooler beside that. "Same goes for the wine. These are usually bottles where the labels are screwed up, or whatever. The product is fine, but we can't sell it. Have you met my brother Kenan?" Blake gestured over toward where Kenan and I were still at the table.

Fiona shook her head as she turned toward us. Kenan stood as she walked with Blake and stopped by the table. He quickly shook her hand. "Good to meet you. Unfortunately, you have to deal with seven family members. Blake is probably the least of your worries," he teased.

Blake rolled his eyes, seeming more relaxed than he had at the interview with Fiona.

"You'll eventually meet all of us," I offered.

"Good to have you," Kenan said.

"Good to see you, Fiona. Everything is delicious," I chimed in.

I watched as she walked out. Blake waited until she had left the room before returning to the table.

When Blake sat down, Kenan slid a sly look in his direction.

"What's that look for?" Blake immediately took the bait.

I chuckled. "Dude, you know better than that."

Blake rolled his eyes. Kenan gave an exaggerated brow waggle. "I know what the deal is."

"What are you talking about?" Blake reached for his plate, adding some seared spicy halibut bites to it before spearing one with his fork and taking a bite.

"You like her," Kenan said.

Blake almost choked on the bite of food he was chewing. I pushed a bottle of water toward him. Glancing at Kenan, I offered, "I think you have a point."

Blake took a swallow of water and cleared his throat. "I definitely don't."

"How much should we bet?" Kenan directed his question to me.

"No way. I'm not betting on that."

"He bet on you and Haven." Kenan thumbed toward Blake.

"You guys bet on Haven and me?"

Blake shrugged. "Sure. Why not?"

I looked back at Kenan. "I'm in. Hundred bucks says Blake can't admit it."

Blake sputtered, pressing his tongue into the side of his cheek as he glared at us. "I don't even like her."

"You definitely can't keep your eyes off her. I noticed at the interview that you were off your game. Flirting comes as easy as breathing to you, and you don't even flirt with her." I gestured toward him with my fork before taking a bite.

"It's not professional to flirt with anyone at an interview. Now, she works for us, so it's even more unprofessional for me to flirt."

Kenan set his fork down, taking a slow pull from his beer. He studied Blake as he lowered the bottle to the table again. "Dude, that's great you're so professional, but you're a flirt. Also, David's her direct boss, not you. You're all tense around her. Mark my words. I'm right about this."

Blake rolled his eyes, glancing at me. "I lost the bet, by the way."

"When you voted on Haven and me?" He nodded. "What was the bet?"

"How long you two would stay together. I really thought it would last. How are you holding up?"

Kenan looked back and forth between us as he chewed. After he finished, he asked, "What am I missing? I thought you and Haven were back on?"

"We were. Then she saw Cathy hitting on me. Nothing happened." I took a bite, chewing furiously as if I could get my frustration out on the poor piece of food.

"It's not just that. Rhys dropped off the recycling one morning and found two pregnancy test boxes. Haven's pregnant and hadn't told him yet," Blake summarized quickly. "Hope you don't mind me filling in that blank." A brow hitched up as he glanced over at me.

I finished chewing and shrugged. "That sums it up."

"Fuck. I guess I'd be a little thrown too. So who dumped who?" Kenan asked.

"Me, I guess. If she was going to dump me over

seeing Cathy flirt with me, I didn't give her a chance. I'm salty that she couldn't even be bothered to tell me she thought she was pregnant."

"To ask the obvious question, what do you use for birth control?" Kenan asked as he rested his elbows on the table before reaching for a savory roll. He took a bite, letting out a moan. As soon as he finished chewing, he glanced toward Blake. "I don't care what you think. This food is fucking amazing. This is just a roll." He held up the half roll that was left. "It's stuffed with some kind of cheese and ham and spices. It shouldn't be that amazing."

"Agreed." I glanced at Kenan. "Haven's on the pill, but nothing's for sure."

Kenan chewed on the other half of his roll as Blake replied, "Shit. You hear about things like that, but don't worry about it. How long has she known?"

I shrugged. "I don't know precisely. I think a week or so."

"Does she want the baby?" Kenan followed that bomb of a question by finishing off his beer and spinning the bottle between his fingers when he set it on the table.

"That's a hell of a question. I don't even know. I didn't give her a chance to tell me. What the fuck should I do?" I set my fork down and leaned back in my chair, looking between my brothers.

"You love Haven, right?" Blake prompted.

My heart tumbled unsteadily in my chest as I nodded.

"Are you with her in this no matter what?" Kenan asked, his sharp gaze studying me.

Chapter Thirty-Seven

HAVEN

I stared at the flames flickering in the woodstove, trying to ignore the sharp ache in my chest. Missing Rhys was a visceral feeling. I just wanted to talk to him. I thought it made sense to give him space, but I missed the sound of his voice, the way his eyes crinkled a little at the corners with his smile, and the warmth of his touch. Just him.

As the days passed, I started to feel I'd overreacted about Cathy. I'd let my own insecurities crowd out everything else.

I knew he was hurt that I hadn't told him I might be pregnant. I'd figured why panic about something if it wasn't real? What if I hadn't been pregnant?

Again and again, my eyes were pulled toward his house. The windows were dark. He hadn't been there in days, not that I could tell. I wanted to text him and ask where he was. My best guess was he was staying with one of his brothers, or maybe he'd traveled to Juneau for business. The minute I thought of Juneau, I reached for my phone. It had been a few weeks since

I'd talked to my mom. I needed some clear advice and trusted her to give it to me.

I slid my thumb across my phone screen to call her. As soon as I heard her voice, I almost burst into tears.

"Haven?" my mother prompted.

"Hey, Mom." I swiped the tears away from my cheeks and sniffled.

"Honey, what's wrong? You sound like you're crying."

I sighed and sniffled again. "I guess I am. I'm pregnant."

"Oh!" My mother's tone rose sharply with her surprise. "I'm guessing this is a surprise for you as well."

"Yeah." I had my tears under control. "I'm on birth control, but I guess things happen. I wasn't ready to talk to Rhys about it because I didn't know what I wanted to do. When I took a pregnancy test, I wasn't even sure if I was pregnant so I thought maybe it was nothing, just nothing to worry about." I sucked in a deep breath of air.

"Is he upset with you?" she asked gently.

I swallowed through the achy knot of emotion in my throat. "Yeah. It's been a weird couple of months. You know I broke up with him before?"

"I know, and I understood why. You have some challenges with trust, but I thought you two were working your way past that." My mother's tone was level but gentle.

"We were. But Cathy, the one who filed the child support paperwork, came here with her son. He's Jake's son. I guess I just let my own insecurities get in the way. She's really beautiful."

I could practically imagine my mother's face right

now. Her lips would press together, and she would eye me over her glasses.

"Honey, you're beautiful."

"I'm your daughter. You're supposed to think that," I protested.

"Maybe so. I won't argue the point. I've seen Rhys with you. He really loves you. I think you both have some baggage that's getting in your way. Rhys doesn't trust the universe because his family has been through some painful events, and you don't trust men. What do you want?"

"For things to be okay with Rhys," I said softly.

"Well, make sure he knows that and give it a little time. Do you want the baby?"

I let out a snort. "I can't believe I'm saying this, but yes. It's not that I didn't think I eventually wanted children. I did. But this feels out of the blue. Now things are weird with Rhys, and I keep thinking that should make me question it, but it's not."

"Having children is never easy. Listen to your heart on this."

"Do you mind if I go to the cabin for a few days?" I asked impulsively. "You could meet me there."

My parents had a small, cozy cabin my dad had used for hunting. He didn't hunt much anymore, but they'd made some improvements to it. Since it was only about an hour and a half drive out of Fireweed Harbor, it was a great getaway. My mother would need to take the ferry to get there, but I could drive.

I craved my mother's steady, warm presence. I needed something to center me, and maybe she could do that. I also wanted my father's quieter but just as calm and centering company. My mother tended to be the one I talked to and felt closer to, but my father was just as important. He was a solid, stabilizing force in our family, like the foundation of a house, I suppose. Maybe it wasn't frilly, and you didn't decorate it, but it was as important as everything else.

"You know you're welcome anytime. I was just saying to your father this morning that we should take the ferry up there for a visit. Sometimes when something startling happens, we all just need a little time. When would you like to meet there? I can check with work and take the ferry the day after tomorrow."

"I have to work tomorrow, but I'll leave afterward. I'll bring you some goodies from the bakery."

"We'd love that. I also need a new mug from Spill the Beans Café. The handle on mine broke."

I was smiling after I ended the call a few minutes later. This was what I needed. It certainly wouldn't solve all my problems, but it would help. It would also keep me from obsessing over the dark windows at Rhys's house.

The following evening, I snagged my backpack out of the break room. I had already packed for the weekend. Phyllis was standing in the kitchen. She held up a box. "Here. I know your mom loves the cranberry-orange scones. There are some of those, along with your father's favorite oatmeal molasses cookies. I also put two mugs in here for your mom."

"Phyllis, let me pay for this stuff. Please."

"No," Phyllis said firmly. "Your mother is a dear friend. You tell her I expect to see her in the next few months." I smiled as I took the box from Phyllis. She leaned up and kissed my cheek. "Have a safe trip. We'll see you when you get back."

I loved the drive from Fireweed Harbor to my parents' cabin. My parents had moved to Juneau when my father had taken a position with the University of

Alaska. They'd sold their old house here, but they'd kept the cabin.

Tomorrow was the third day since I had texted Rhys. I was going to be restless until then, so a getaway was a good plan. As I drove, I admired the views of the ocean, mountains, and glaciers. The sun was setting, creating a splashy watercolor in the sky with a swirl of bright reds and oranges. I kept the windows in the back cracked. It was spring and still chilly out, but the air smelled so good.

I got the last lingering colors of the sun for the first few minutes before it slipped behind the mountains, and the stars and the moon claimed the sky, glittering in the darkness.

The communities in Southeast Alaska weren't connected by roads since mountains and glaciers surrounded them. Each area had its own road system for any local travel. When my headlights illuminated a sign announcing a detour due to construction, I assumed I could easily navigate it. I didn't think much of it and followed the signs onto a side road off the highway. I was startled by a moose abruptly bolting into the road and slammed on my brakes, muttering, "Close call."

When I didn't see another sign guiding me back toward the highway, I started to get a little worried. The road I was on transitioned from pavement to gravel.

"Nothing unusual," I said to myself.

Alaska had plenty of gravel roads. Even sections of the main highways in the less settled areas were gravel for miles upon miles. The road curved ahead, and I followed it, thinking, *This makes sense. This must be parallel to the highway.*

Or so I thought. A solid half hour later, I stared at the orange sign mounted in the road. *End of road.*

I glared at the sign. "What the fuck?"

I glanced down at my phone. Of course, I had no reception. I also glared at that and my car's useless GPS. This was not good. I'd been planning to get gas on the highway.

And, now, my best guess was I was deep into Tongass National Forest. I hadn't seen lights from a house in at least twenty minutes. There was no way I was getting out and walking anywhere.

Putting my car in park, I clambered into the back seat and reached into the hatch, dragging my emergency kit forward. I had a nice winter sleeping bag and a few supplies. For better or worse, I could make it through the night.

Looking at my phone again, I willed some kind of signal to come forth. Eyeing my gas gauge, I knew I had a few miles that I could go and maybe that would bring me closer to a signal. According to the gauge, I had thirty miles worth of gas. I had easily driven thirty miles along this detour. I didn't even know how the hell that happened. I started driving back, checking my phone signal every minute or so.

As soon as I got one bar, I pulled over, my headlights arcing out over what appeared to be a small valley.

Please, please, please.

My mother's phone rang three times before she picked up. "Mom!" I exclaimed. "I'm lost. There's a detour and—" The line went dead.

Lowering my phone, I stared at the screen. *Call dropped.*

When I tried to call my mother again, the call was dropped before the phone even rang.

Chapter Thirty-Eight

RHYS

As I walked up the stairs at my house, I couldn't keep myself from looking over at Haven's place. Not a single light was on, and her car wasn't outside.

This was the first night I'd come home in the past two days. I'd offered to help Adam out with the house he was building just down the road from where I intended to construct a place soon. It was easier to stay out there, or so I'd told myself.

Once I was inside the house, I opened my refrigerator. "Fuck," I muttered.

I needed to go grocery shopping. My phone vibrated in my pocket as I released the refrigerator door, letting it fall shut. Sliding my phone out of my pocket, I glanced at the screen to see Deacon's name and answered the call immediately. "Hey, Deacon, what's up?"

"Haven is lost," he barked in my ear.

"What?!" My stomach dropped. "What the hell are you talking about?"

"My mom just called me. She said Haven was driving to the cabin. She said a few other things.

Apparently, neither one of you can be bothered to keep me up to speed. Maybe your relationship is none of my business, but she's my sister," he said pointedly.

"Deacon, where is Haven?" I ground out. "You can give me hell later."

"Point taken. All I know is she left after work today. My mom didn't know there was construction on the highway because of that rock slide last winter. Remember?"

"Yeah." Dread and worry tightened in my gut.

"Haven called her to tell her there was a detour, but the call got dropped. My mom has tried to call her back, but she can't get through to her. Based on when she left, Haven should've been there over an hour ago at this point. My mom called the state troopers, and they said they can go out there and try to find Haven. She's on that stretch between Fireweed Harbor and the national forest. The closest trooper is at least an hour and a half away."

I was already walking out of the house. "I'm on my way. I'll call my brothers and McKenna, and we'll all start looking. Where are you?"

"In Fairbanks. I checked the flight schedule, and there are no flights from here to Fireweed Harbor until early tomorrow morning."

"I'm on it. I'll call you. If you can get a line in to the firefighters here, maybe they can give us some info about the detour route."

"You got it. I'll text you."

My heart crashed against my ribs, panic, and fear banging together like loud cymbals. I called Blake first as I began driving.

"Haven's lost," I said as soon as he answered.

I could hear the familiar muted cacophony from the winery in the background. "What?"

"She was driving to her parents' cabin outside of town. We don't know what happened except she called her mom and said there was a detour and she was lost. The call dropped, and no one can reach her. She should've been there over an hour ago."

"Fuck. Give me five minutes, and I'll be ready to leave. Do you want me to ride with you?"

"That'd be great." Worried as I was, I knew Haven was sensible. She wouldn't leave her car. I *knew* that. I clung to that hope. "I'm driving right over to get you."

After that, I called Kenan and Adam. Conveniently, Kenan was with Adam. They said they would start driving right away.

Blake had already called McKenna. She texted me as I was pulling into the parking lot behind the winery.

I called her back while I waited for Blake to come out. "Do you want me to drive down there?" she asked by way of greeting.

My mind spun through the options. "I don't think so. Blake and I are leaving now, and Adam and Kenan are also on their way. Why don't you call Deacon and be his point of contact? He said he's going to touch base with the fire station here and see if they can get us a map of wherever the detour is supposed to go and where she could've ended up."

"You got it." I started to hang up, stopping when McKenna added, "Rhys?"

"Yeah?"

"Haven will be okay."

"I hope so." That was all I could manage in return.

My chest literally ached. Dread settled in a cold ball in my stomach. Haven was sensible, and I knew she would stay in her car. I just hoped she hadn't gotten too far off course. Cell reception was spotty in the mountains and forests covering Southeast Alaska.

A moment later, Blake was opening the door to my SUV. "Let's go," he said.

He buckled his seat belt in a flash, and I started driving. When I came to the stop sign to turn onto the highway, he asked, "Do you want me to drive?"

Glancing sideways, I met his concerned gaze. "Nah. I'll lose my mind just sitting there."

The first few minutes of the drive were quiet.

"Haven will be fine." Blake's clear and firm voice was filled with certainty.

"I hope so." I took a breath, willing the reckless beat of my heart to settle. I wasn't typically an anxious guy, but right now, anxiety had my pulse kicking along at an unsteady beat and dread coating my insides.

My cell phone rang, the dashboard screen lighting up with Deacon's name. I tapped it to answer. "Hey, Blake is with me, and you're on speaker."

"Hey, Blake," Deacon said quickly. "The troopers are on their way, but the two closest ones on duty are farther away than you are. They just finished dealing with a car accident north of Fireweed Harbor. I spoke to one of the firefighters in Fireweed Harbor. He told me the detour loops through part of the national forest. He said there are signs, but it sounds like she missed them. He assures me it comes to a dead end in the forest if she missed the signs to turn. There aren't many side roads. I'm going to text you the map he sent me."

"Text it to Blake. I'm driving. Actually, text it to all of us. Adam and Kenan should be behind us any minute now."

"They've already texted me," Blake chimed in.

"Looks like they're only a few miles behind us. Adam is driving."

"Got it."

"How much of the main highway is blocked?" I asked.

"It's about a five-mile stretch. When that rock slide happened last winter, it knocked off the side of the road along that area with the steep bluff. They're going to repair it soon. The firefighter crew will head out as well. I'm sure you guys will find her."

"I have my satellite phone," Blake said, lifting it from beside his feet. I hadn't even noticed he had it with him.

Blake and I both enjoyed backcountry skiing, so we had satellite phones for when we went out to more isolated areas. I just hadn't been thinking to get my gear when I left.

"Good call," Deacon replied. "All right, guys. You keep driving. Call me once you find her."

"You've got some faith," I returned.

"Of course I do."

After we ended the call, my phone vibrated where it sat in the console. "Check that for me."

"It's the map," Blake said.

He tapped his phone screen and widened his fingers to enlarge the view.

"Haven's going to be fine," I said, almost as if to myself.

"We're gonna find her." Blake sounded confident, more confident than I felt.

"It's dark and..." My eyes flicked to the dashboard screen. "It's just over thirty degrees out."

Nights in Alaska were cool in the spring. It would drop to freezing at the higher elevations for another month at least. I didn't want to think about the fact that people were more likely to get hypothermia when the temperature hovered above freezing. Because the human body needed to stay warmer than just above freezing, a lot warmer.

I hoped Haven had plenty of gas to keep her car warm.

"Have you talked to her in the last few days?" Blake asked.

"Since I found out she was pregnant?"

"Yeah. I know you're upset. I get it. But—"

I cut in. "I know. I should've talked to her. Right now, I just want to find her. I'm hurt that she didn't tell me, but I love her. That's all that really matters."

"It is." Blake paused, taking a swallow from his water bottle. "Speaking of people not telling us things, Cathy flew out early."

"She did?" I was frankly relieved to have the distraction of something else to talk about.

"She was supposed to leave in two days, but she called Mom and said something came up with work. Mom said she thinks she'll stay in touch."

"I think she will. Maybe she wanted more child support for Matthew, but Mom just wants to be in contact with Matthew like any grandmother. In Mom's ideal world, Cathy would live here so Mom could see Matthew every day, but that's not going to happen."

"Yeah," Blake said dryly. "I think it's for the best there will be a little distance. This way, she can just love him, visit him, and won't get all tied up wishing she could bring Jake back."

I took a breath, letting it out slowly. "I think you're right."

"Has Haven told you if she wants to keep the baby?"

"Because I'm an idiot, I didn't really give her a chance to talk about it."

"What do you think now?"

My eyes stung with tears, and my throat felt tight. I forced myself to take a slow breath. "I love her, and I just want it to work out."

"How do you feel about being a father?" Blake wasn't going to let me slide.

"I've actually had some time to think about that recently," I said with a sharp, humorless laugh. "I kind of panicked when I thought maybe Matthew was my son, but I'm not panicking now. I think you were right."

"About what?"

"When you said I was holding something back."

When I slid a quick look at my brother, he wasn't laughing or teasing. His gaze was somber as he nodded. "We've got each other, but our family's got some shit to deal with. We all have our reasons to hold back."

"We do. We're going to find Haven, and I'm going to make sure she knows I love her. If she wants to have our baby, I'm there. One hundred percent."

Blake reached over, squeezing my shoulder lightly before his hand dropped away. "You'll be a good father. You've had to be a father to all of us at times."

"Dude, I'm only a year and a half older than you." I tried to tease because this conversation felt heavy, and my emotions crested high.

"Still."

My throat felt tight again when I reached for the water bottle tucked in the side of the door. "Let's find Haven."

Chapter Thirty-Nine

HAVEN

I burrowed deeper into my down coat, clenching my jaw in an effort to keep my teeth from chattering. I had resorted to periodically starting my car and blasting the heat for a few minutes, just enough to break through the cold before turning it back off. My gas gauge told me I only had twenty miles left. Seeing as I didn't know when someone would come by, I needed to make it through the night.

My winter emergency kit contained a winter sleeping bag, one of those emergency blankets, first-aid flares, and so on. I still debated whether it was worth using a flare out here. I tried to remember the last house I'd driven past, but I wasn't sure.

I knew I had to have traveled into the forestry roads. Tongass National Forest stretched along the side of the highway outside of Fireweed Harbor.

"I'll make it through the night," I whispered.

I would. I didn't want to be cold, and I knew this weather was perilous. I had to stay warm. I could do it. But I would be bored and lonely and trying to fend off my fear all night.

My mind kept circling back to Rhys. It all seemed so rational to take a few days to give him space. Yet now, the ache of missing him was painfully sharp. I felt almost breathless if I let myself think about him for too long.

In the dark, cold night, my insecurities around Cathy felt silly. My surprise pregnancy felt too much. The timing was terrible, and I knew it. Yet I still wanted our baby. I had no idea what Rhys wanted.

A tear rolled down my cheek, and I swiped it away with my hand. I immediately stuffed my hand back in my pocket, only to have another roll down my other cheek. I blinked fiercely before freeing both hands from my pockets and opening the glove box to grab a tissue. I quickly blew my nose and dried my eyes. I didn't need to be a weepy mess while I waited lost on some gravel road in the darkness.

I glanced at my phone. I was keeping it on. Blessedly, it was fully charged before I last turned my car off. It was now approaching midnight.

My mom had to have called someone by this point. I just hoped they could find me. I told myself they would. They had to.

Time ticked by. When I shivered all over, I stuffed myself in my winter sleeping bag in the front seat and ate the muffins I'd brought to give to my mother. I'd have to remember to replenish the small food supply in my emergency kit because all I'd had in there was a stale granola bar.

After checking my phone again and willing some kind of signal to appear, I let out a sigh. When I'd first parked, I'd gotten out of my car and climbed on top of it, holding the phone high to see if I could get a signal. I'd deemed it too risky to walk in any direction in the darkness, knowing that I hadn't had a signal for miles.

This area was spotty for cell phone reception, even on the highway. The mountains weren't helpful.

I was starting to get warm in my winter sleeping bag when I saw headlights flickering through the trees in the distance. They didn't seem to be on this road. I debated starting my car and following them, but I didn't know where I was and didn't want to get more lost.

"Please, please, please, please, please," I whispered in the darkness, my breath puffing in the air with every word.

The moon high in the sky illuminated the inside of my car. I debated whether to start my car again when I saw headlights in the distance. On this very road.

I almost burst into tears. I held my emotion in check and started the car, turning on my lights to flash them repeatedly. Then I turned my car back off immediately.

I waited.

It felt like forever, but it must've only been a few minutes before the vehicle reached me. As soon as I saw the shape of it, I knew it was Rhys. I fumbled with the zipper on my sleeping bag. He was at my car before I could even get it all the way unzipped. I burst into tears the moment he opened the door.

His concerned gaze coasted over my face quickly. "Are you okay?"

I nodded through my tears. He helped me out of my sleeping bag and pulled me into his arms. Pressing my face into his neck, I breathed him in through my tears, crying a little harder at his familiar scent. His embrace was warm and strong.

I faintly heard Blake's voice nearby and another vehicle pulling up, barely noticing that Adam and Kenan were also here.

I heard Rhys talking to various people, but he held me close as I clung to him. An emergency vehicle arrived within a few minutes. Only then did he set me back, saying, "You're shivering hard. We need to have them check you over."

I shook my head, but he insisted. I was hiccupping and sniffling while a woman asked me several questions. My temperature was a little below normal. I heard Rhys swear.

"You need to go to the hospital," he ordered.

The woman glanced over, saying, "She just needs to be somewhere warm."

I looked around blearily. The relief of having Rhys here and knowing I would be okay finally sank in. Blake stood beside Rhys with one hand in his pocket as he said something to Adam.

Kenan came over and held a thermos out. "We thought ahead. Hot chocolate," he said.

He started to hand me the thermos, but Rhys reached for it. "Is there alcohol in that?"

Kenan glanced at him. "Uh, no. Is there a problem if there is?"

"She's pregnant," Rhys bit out.

Adam and Kenan looked my way together, Adam appearing almost comically surprised.

Blake glanced over at me. "He told me the news. Congratulations, I think."

"Whoa," Adam finally said.

Before I could even protest it, Rhys started insisting we had to go to the hospital.

The EMT leaned in, asking, "Do you know how far along you are?"

"I think about seven weeks."

She nodded. "She doesn't need to go to the hospital." She glanced at Rhys. "Get her somewhere warm and keep her warm tonight. That's the treatment for hypothermia, but she's not dangerously cold yet."

The brothers conferred about how to deal with my car. Adam and Kenan had planned ahead. They even had a full gas can. I was about to argue the point about driving it home, but Rhys wouldn't hear of it. They decided Blake would drive my car back to Fireweed Harbor. Rhys would drive me, and Adam and Kenan would follow.

A short while later, after we got into cell range, I called my mother and updated her. When I lowered the phone, I glanced at Rhys.

"I can stay at my place if that's best."

His gaze slid to mine. The intensity in his eyes, even in the dim light cast from his dashboard, nearly took my breath away. "I'm taking you home. With me."

Chapter Forty

RHYS

Emotion was crashing through me, one wave after another. My heart banged against my ribs as I drove, my hands gripping the steering wheel tightly. I almost didn't trust myself to talk, but I knew I needed to.

"I'm sorry," Haven blurted out.

"You don't need to apologize. I was upset because you didn't tell me, but—" I took a quick breath before continuing. "I understand. You didn't expect to be pregnant, and if it turned out to be negative, it would've been nothing. I love you. I really do." I paused for another steadying breath. "I understand, maybe, why you had your doubts about us."

Haven interjected, asking, "Can I say something?"

"Of course."

"The thing with Cathy, it's just my insecurities. I don't have any other excuse. I should've trusted you. You did nothing to make me doubt you."

I glanced over at her. "I appreciate that, but I think maybe I did. Not about Cathy specifically." My heart crashed against my ribs again and again as anxiety spun in my chest. "You know my family story.

It's messy. I knew I loved you, but I didn't realize or didn't grasp that I hadn't let myself be vulnerable. I was determined to show you I loved you by being the perfect guy. When what I needed to do was just be a little more..." I paused, shaking my head. "I don't even know how to explain it. I just think maybe I was pulling back a little bit, not because the feelings weren't there but because that's been my whole life."

When I slid my gaze sideways to look at Haven, a sheen of tears shone in her eyes. "I didn't mean to upset you," I said quickly.

She reached for one of my hands where it rested on the edge of the steering wheel. I let go and laced my fingers through hers. "It's not that. Your family has been through a lot. You are all so close now, and things are solid with your mom, so sometimes I can forget what it means. Your dad died, and Jake died. Then there's what you went through with your grandfather, all of you. It's really sad. You had to be the strong one for a long time."

I took a shaky breath as I nodded, keeping my eyes focused on the road.

"Then all the stuff with not knowing if I was Matthew's father." I shook my head. "It kind of all tangled together. I love you. I'm not perfect, but you have nothing to worry about with Cathy or anyone."

"I'm sorry I doubted you."

I glanced over, shrugging. "I understand why you did. Not like I was an ass, but before you, I never let anybody in." She squeezed my hand again. "What do you want to do?"

"About what?" she asked in return.

"You're pregnant. Now, more people than maybe you wanted to know about that know."

She laughed softly. "That's okay. I'm a little

surprised, but I want to keep our baby. But I'm not sure how you feel about that."

"If you want our baby, I do too. I've had some time to think about being a father lately," I offered dryly.

"I think a baby is a little different."

"True, but I'm just saying. This is how I would want it to be. With you. Us."

———

When we got home, I needed Haven in a way I never had before. Once we were in the house, I cupped her face as I looked down. "I love you," I whispered.

I kissed her, meaning for it to be gentle, but it wasn't. Not at all. I devoured her mouth as her tongue tangled with mine. By the time we broke apart, we were both breathless, gulping in air.

Haven stared back at me, her breath coming in sharp heaves. I ran my hands down her arms. "Are you warm enough?" I asked.

She nodded quickly. "I'm fine."

I opened my mouth to say something, something along the lines of telling her we should slow down, that we didn't have to rush, that...

She leaned forward, pressing a hot, open-mouthed kiss in the divot at the base of my throat. Her touch felt like a drop of warm honey on my skin, rippling through my system in hot shocks. I slipped my hand around the back of her head, holding her close.

"This can wait." My voice came out gruff as emotion trampled through me, and my heart kicked against my ribs.

She leaned back slightly, peering up at me. "I don't want to wait."

When I stepped back, my hand fell away. She

caught it, lacing her fingers through mine and giving me a little tug. "Let's take a shower."

Moments later, hot water rained down around us. I couldn't keep my hands off Haven. Bubbles rolled over her skin. Moments later, I'd pressed my hands flat against the tiled wall. I kissed Haven as if she were the very air I needed to breathe. One of her hands mapped my chest as she reached between us, curling her other hand around my insistent arousal. I was swollen to the point of pain.

I gasped into our kiss before breaking free and sucking in a deep breath. "Haven," I bit out. "This isn't just sex for me. I need you to know that. I love you."

Her palm rested just above my heart. She pressed firmly, my heart pounding harder in response. "I love you too," she whispered. "I know it's not just about that. I need to explain."

I slid my hand down her side, hooking my palm under her knee. "No, you don't."

She blinked before leaning up to kiss me. I held her close, lifting her knee higher and adjusting the angle of my hips as I sank home.

This time, when she shuddered and cried my name, my heart felt cracked open, split wide as the lightning of my own release sizzled through my system.

A short while later, we were eating pizza from Fire-weed Winery, and Haven was bundled in a pair of my sweatpants and a fleece shirt. Her legs rested on my knees with the pizza box on her lap while we ate from it.

We *had* talked. I had explained I finally understood I held a piece of myself back because I knew what it meant to lose someone. Because maybe I had learned in my messy family story that pain was part of the ties that bound us all together, and it was easier to keep a part of myself separate.

She blinked up at me after I dumped my heart out in words and trailed her fingertips along my jawline before her hand slipped down to rest over my heart again. I watched her take a deep breath, her gaze soft.

"That makes sense. For me, I think I just couldn't believe you really wanted me. My only other serious relationship wasn't a tragedy, but I struggled with trust. In high school, I felt like I never fit in."

I cut in. "Haven, you're beautiful. I'm not just saying that."

Her lips curled slightly at the corners. "I always imagined someone like Cathy being the kind of girl you would fall for. You *did* sort of have a relationship with her."

I shrugged. "I wouldn't call it a relationship. I was in college, and we enjoyed each other for a few weekends. I was shallow then, and so was she. I'm not that guy anymore and haven't been for years. There's literally nothing there with her. I'm kind of embarrassed there ever was. She did try to push for something, but there was never *any* risk of that happening. Even if I wasn't completely in love with you."

She leaned forward once again, dropping another kiss right at the base of my throat before leaning back. "Well, we've sorted all that out."

My chuckle was dry. "We have." As the laughter faded, a lingering jolt of fear struck me. "I was terrified tonight until we found you."

"I was prepared," she insisted. "You saw my giant sleeping bag."

"I know, but things could've gone wrong."

"But they didn't," she whispered, her palm circling over my heart.

I took a breath as I nodded. I slid my palm over her belly. "So?"

She leaned her forehead to mine, curling her hand over mine.

EPILOGUE

Haven

A year or so later

I pushed through heavy layers of sleep before bolting upright in bed. I looked around the room wildly. Rhys wasn't in bed with me, and little Jake's crib was empty.

Once you had a baby, I quickly learned that a sense of panic built when you didn't know where your baby was. I scrambled out of bed, running barefoot out to the living room. Rhys was in the kitchen, talking in a low voice to our baby boy Jake. Once we knew he was a boy, we both knew we wanted to name him Jake after Rhys's brother.

Rhys poured a cup of coffee with one hand and turned when I came skidding to a stop by the counter. I wore one of his T-shirts, which hung to the tops of my thighs. He smiled over at me.

"Good morning." He finished pouring the coffee and set the pot down on the burner before turning and crossing over to me. He gave me a lingering kiss while Jake let out a happy gurgle when he saw me.

My heart felt as if it was going to burst out of my chest at the sound. The sheer unadulterated joy with which a baby greeted you elicited a mirroring response inside.

"Hey, sweet boy," I said, smoothing my hand over his hair. I looked up at Rhys. "I can't believe I slept through him waking up."

Rhys grinned. "I can. He didn't sleep well last night, so you didn't either."

"That means neither did you," I pointed out.

He shrugged. "I wasn't going to wake you up when you were still asleep this morning. We take our sleep when we can get it," he said lightly.

Never in my life had I lost as much sleep as I had in the first few months after having Jake. I knew I would adjust, and he was starting to have better nights, but holy hell. Sometimes I just dragged myself through the days. I was profoundly grateful I worked at a coffee shop.

Rhys was nudging me to let that job go, pointing out that it wasn't like I needed the money. Although it was intimidating to marry into a family that was billionaire wealthy, they were all so down to earth and worked hard.

Rhys didn't expect me to quit and twiddle my thumbs. Meanwhile, McKenna was lobbying for me to work full-time with them. I planned to keep my existing online graphics business, but they had plenty of work to give me at Fireweed Industries. Deciding on that was for another day.

For now, I smiled up at Rhys, still marveling that we had a baby. We had decided to get married before I had the baby. Not because we had to but because we wanted to. Even though I made wedding invitations for other people and was aware of how much some people loved the idea of a big wedding, I didn't want that. I wanted something small.

Because our first encounter since high school was in the house Rhys was staying in and where we still lived, we had a small ceremony here in the backyard during the summer and had the reception at Spill the Beans Café.

Rhys poured me a cup of coffee. I nursed Jake for a few minutes, and he promptly fell asleep. After I put him back in his crib for a nap, we enjoyed our coffee in the kitchen while Rhys made scrambled eggs. It was all very mundane. I loved it.

He reached for my hand when I pushed my plate away, lightly lifting it to turn it over and drop a kiss in the center of my palm. The sensation sent little ripples of heat rolling through me.

"Do you work today?" he asked.

When I shook my head, his gaze darkened. "Excellent. Come here then."

Before I knew it, he had pulled me onto his lap and had his way with me in the kitchen. When you had a baby, you stole every moment you could when they came along.

When it was all over but the gasping, he leaned back, his eyes skating over me. "I told you I would make you mine," he whispered, that wicked flame still lingering in his gaze.

Thank you for reading Rhys & Haven's story! Want a glimpse of the future for them? Join my newsletter to receive an exclusive scene.

Sign up here: https://BookHip.com/KZFSSQT

p.s. If you are already subscribed, you'll still be able to access the scene.

Up next in the Fireweed Harbor Series is Dare To Fall.

Fiona is uptight, delectably distracting, *and* she works for my family. I make one rule for myself: hands off.

Once, just *once*, I break my own rule. After that, Fiona becomes my secret.

Don't miss Fiona & Blake's story - it's swoony, forbidden & sweet!

Pre-order Dare To Fall - due out June 12, 2023!

For more swoony romance...

This Crazy Love kicks off the Swoon Series - small town southern romance with enough heat to melt you! Jackson & Shay's story is epic - swoon-worthy & intensely emotional. Jackson just happens to be Shay's brother's best friend. He's also *seriously* easy on the eyes. Shay has a past, the kind of past she would most definitely like to forget. Past or not, Jackson is about to rock her world. Don't miss their story! Free on all retailers!

Burn For Me is a second chance romance for the ages. Sexy firefighters? Check. Rugged men? Check. Wrapped up together? Check. Brave the fire in this hot, small-town romance. Amelia & Cade were high school sweethearts & then it all fell apart. When they cross paths again, it's epic - don't miss Cade's story! Free on all retailers!

For more small town romance, take a visit to Last Frontier Lodge in Diamond Creek. A sexy, alpha SEAL

meets his match with a brainy heroine in Take Me Home. Marley is all brains & Gage is all brawn. Sparks fly when their worlds collide. Don't miss Gage & Marley's story!
Free on all retailers!

If sports romance lights your spark, check out The Play. Liam is a British footballer who falls for Olivia, his doctor. A twist of forbidden heats up this swoon-worthy & laugh-out-loud romance. Don't miss Liam & Olivia's story.
Free on all retailers!

FIND MY BOOKS

Thank you for reading Make You Mine! I hope you enjoyed the story. If so, you can help other readers find my books in a variety of ways.

1) Write a review!
2) Sign up for my newsletter, so you can receive information about upcoming new releases & receive a FREE copy of one of my books: http://jhcroixauthor. com/subscribe/
3) Like and follow my Amazon Author page at https:// amazon.com/author/jhcroix
4) Follow me on Bookbub at https://www.bookbub. com/authors/j-h-croix
5) Follow me on Instagram at https://www.instagram. com/jhcroix/
6) Like my Facebook page at https://www.facebook. com/jhcroix

Visit my store to purchase ebooks & fun swag!
J.H. Croix Shop

Fireweed Harbor Series
When We Meet - free prequel!
Make You Mine
Dare To Fall - due out June 2023!
Be The One - due out October 2023!

Light My Fire Series
Wild With You
Hold Me Now
Only Ever Us
Fall For Me
Keep Me Close
With Every Breath
All It Takes
Take Me Now - due out August 2023!
Dare With Me Series
Crash Into You
Evers & Afters
Come To Me
Back To Us
Take Me There
After We Fall
Swoon Series
This Crazy Love
Wait For Me
Break My Fall
Truly Madly Mine
Still Go Crazy
If We Dare
Steal My Heart

Into The Fire Series
Burn For Me
Slow Burn
Burn So Bad
Hot Mess
Burn So Good
Sweet Fire
Play With Fire
Melt With You
Burn For You
Crash & Burn
That Snowy Night
Brit Boys Sports Romance
The Play
Big Win
Out Of Bounds
Play Me
Naughty Wish
Diamond Creek Alaska Novels
When Love Comes
Follow Love
Love Unbroken
Love Untamed
Tumble Into Love
Christmas Nights
Last Frontier Lodge Novels
Take Me Home
Love at Last
Just This Once
Falling Fast
Stay With Me
When We Fall
Hold Me Close
Crazy For You
Just Us

ACKNOWLEDGMENTS

If you made it to the end of this story, THANK YOU!

Gracious thanks to my editor to and Terri D. for helping me make Rhys & Haven's story the best it could be and tidying up the details and those pesky errors. To my early readers for any last details and for loving my stories enough to want them as soon as possible. You have no idea how much that means.

Once again, Najla Qamber spun magic to create the look for this series and gorgeous cover. Much gratitude to the bloggers, bookstagrammers, and booktokers who spread the word about my books and so many others.

My assistant is sooooo much help behind the scenes.

No book would be complete without the support of DBC and my dogs. Much love.

xoxo

J.H. Croix

ABOUT THE AUTHOR

USA Today Bestselling Author J.H. Croix lives in a small town in Maine with her husband and two spoiled dogs. Croix writes contemporary romance with sassy women and alpha men who aren't afraid to show some emotion. Her love for quirky small-towns and the characters that inhabit them shines through in her writing. Take a walk on the wild side of romance with her bestselling novels!

Places you can find me:
jhcroixauthor.com
jhcroix@jhcroix.com

facebook.com/jhcroix
instagram.com/jhcroix
bookbub.com/authors/j-h-croix